GRACE
AND THE SECRET VAULT

A NOVEL

BY

RUTH LATTA

GRACE AND THE SECRET VAULT

© Copyright Ruth Latta – 2016

ISBN 978-1-77216-092-5

Published by:

Baico Publishing Inc.
E-mail: info@baico.ca
Web site: www.baico.ca

ACKNOWLEDGEMENTS

I wish to thank Glenn and Joy Woodsworth for their information and feedback.

Sincere thanks to Evelyn Gigantes, former NDP Member of the Ontario Legislature, and to Lorna Foreman, author and magazine columnist, for reading the manuscript and commenting upon it.

Without my husband's editorial, technical, moral and financial support I would have had great difficulty completing this novel. Thank you, Roger Latta.

CHAPTER ONE

JUNE 1918

When Grace's parents first announced to her and her brothers and sister that they were moving, they were stunned. Moving? Leaving the Landing? Why, they'd only just got here. They had come here to the west coast of Canada in 1917, just over a year ago, and ever since then the children had been having the time of their lives.

Move?

No more running barefoot in the summer? No more fishing off the docks on the waterfront, no more watching boats on Howe Sound, no more trips with Father in the *Goodwill* to the various congregations in his pastoral charge?

No more hikes up the old logging roads into the lush forest with its ferny floor and towering trees? Go away, and never again attend a May Day picnic on one of the Finnish farms up on the flatland overlooking the harbour? Grace and her brothers and sister had such fun at this year's picnic, taking part in the races and other contests, the singing and dancing, and eating the delicious food. Even the baby, Howard, and the second youngest, Bruce, had a good time.

Thirteen year old Grace had two best friends, Anna and Kathy. Mother always said that the friends of your youth were your friends for life, and Grace wanted her friendships here at the Landing to grow and develop. This village on the shore of Howe Sound, twenty miles by water from the city of Vancouver, was a wonderful place, the closest thing to the heaven that Father used to talk about.

Seeing the children's downcast faces, Mother and Father quickly explained that they weren't leaving the Landing. They were moving, yes, but just across town. They would be leaving the Methodist manse and would move into Dr. Fred and Aunt Alice's big new house, Stonehurst. Uncle Fred and Aunt Alice had invited them. It was all arranged.

The little ones clapped their hands. The doctors' children were their favourite playmates. Every child had a "twin" of the same age in the other family. Grace couldn't wait to be living just a flight of stairs away from Kathy.

There was much about the manse the children liked, such as the Dragon Castle, a huge blackened tree, thirty feet high, and hollow, with an opening that all six of them could get into at once. This sort of tree, left over from lumbering days, was called a "stick." But the manse was small and crowded, and Stonehurst was big enough for two families. Also, both sets of parents were good friends and always had much to talk about.

Even if they didn't agree, they respected each other's opinions.

While her younger brothers, Charles and Ralph, talked about learning to ride Uncle Fred's white horse, Paddy, Grace quietly discussed with her sister, Belva, the real reason for the move. It wasn't for the fun of living in the same house as their friends. It was because Father was leaving his job – again.

As the eldest, Grace was the child who helped most with the packing. Often she had to take care of the baby, Howard – known in the family as "the Kid" – while Mother tackled the big tasks. Minding a toddler was hard, because he had to be watched constantly; she couldn't even steal five minutes to read. She was glad when Father asked if he could borrow her to help him pack his books.

Grace loved books, especially novels like *The Call of the Wild* by Jack London, which Father called an "allegory". She had also read *The Water Babies* by Charles Kingsley and *The Ragged Trousered Philanthropists*, by Robert Tressell, and found them absorbing but sad. Some of her father's books were too hard for her at this stage of her life, though later she thought she'd be able to appreciate them – works by the great thinkers like Sidney and Beatrice Webb, William Morris, Friedrich Engels, Karl Marx and others. Every now and then she dipped into these more difficult books to see what she could make of them. Now, she carefully packed them in fruit crates while Father sorted through his old sermons and other papers.

After a while he suggested a break.

"Let's have a little talk," he said.

Conversations with Father sometimes turned out to be one-sided, with he the speaker and she the audience. But this time his opening question didn't sound like the start of a lecture.

"Do you mind that I won't be a preacher any more?" he inquired.

She hesitated, then said, "Not really."

From the time she was a baby, Grace had been going to church, starting in Winnipeg where Father had been an assistant pastor. She liked the Bible stories in Sunday School, and the stained glass windows and the singing, but being a preacher's kid was tiresome, because you always had to be on your best behaviour and be a good example to others.

"How do you feel about living in the upstairs of someone else's house?" Father asked.

"Oh, I really look forward to living at Stonehurst. Of course living in the manse has been fine, too."

Grace had found it fun to come home from school, never knowing which neighbour might be visiting, having a cup of tea and an English lesson. But Uncle Fred's house was a busy one too, and Kathy would be just downstairs.

"That's a relief," Father said. "I worried about upsetting you children, but we can't stay here any longer. Do you understand why we're leaving this house?"

"Because you resigned as minister and we have no right to the manse any more."

"That's right. And do you know why I resigned?" His intense blue eyes met hers.

"I think so." Grace chose her words carefully. "Some of the people who run the church here wanted you to preach in favour of the war and urge men to join the army, and you won't."

He nodded.

"I hope the war will be over soon," she said. "It seems to have been going on forever."

The Great War had started back in 1914 when Grace was only nine. That summer, the Archduke of Austria was shot in Serbia. The great powers of Europe took sides, with Germany supporting Austria and Russia supporting Serbia. Great Britain and France were allied with Russia, so they declared war on Germany. Since Canada was part of the British Empire, she automatically went to war when Great Britain did.

But Grace had heard adults say that the assassination of the archduke was just an excuse, that for a long time, the leaders of Germany and Britain had been racing each other to colonize Africa and expand their empires, and itching to fight.

Grace remembered the excitement when war was declared. Soldiers paraded, Union Jacks waved, stirring band music played. Young men couldn't wait to get into uniform to join the Canadian Expeditionary Force and go overseas to "fight the Hun." What an adventure, to help out the Mother Country! They were sure that Britain and her allies would defeat the armies of Germany's Kaiser Wilhelm in no time at all, and that they'd be back home, victorious and rejoicing, by

Christmas 1914. But it was now the spring of 1918 and the war was still going on.

Back in 1914, Father was forty years old, close to the age at which men were considered too old to join the army. He was head of a government-funded social welfare organization, finding help for people in need, including many newcomers to Canada. As part of his work he organized a training course for social workers and travelled from Winnipeg to other cities to learn about the social programs they offered and to speak on the need for programs to aid struggling, suffering people. Mother explained to the children that Father, formerly a church minister, had found a new pastorate, one that was nation-wide. Grace remembered going with him to his office downtown, along with Belva and Charles, to help him with a mailing. The three children had glued stamps to hundreds of letters. She'd been around ten at the time. Father had left this job, too, because of the war.

He seemed to be reading her mind, for he broke the silence by asking if she knew why they'd left Winnipeg.

"Yes," she said. "So many soldiers were getting killed in Europe that the Ottawa government decided to register all the men in the country who were of the age to serve in the army. You knew this registration was the first step toward making them go overseas to fight, and your conscience wouldn't allow let you go along with it, so you quit."

"That's it in a nutshell. You're a perceptive girl, Grace."

"Well, I'm glad you took a stand," she said. "I wouldn't want to be sent across the ocean to live in a trench and be bombarded with shells. I hate the people who beat the drum for the war."

Father shook his head. "You mustn't hate. Hate is what caused this terrible war – hate and greed. Now, the end may be in sight. The Americans have come in to help Britain and France. But let's not talk about the war. Have you any questions about our move?"

Grace hesitated. "Just one thing. The Methodist Church won't be paying you a salary any more, so what will we live on?"

"We have a few dollars put aside," Father said. "Also, your mother will be earning money. She's been asked to teach this coming fall. You'll have her for French and some other subjects."

Grace beamed. "I'm so glad! I'll be the perfect student and not cause her any trouble."

Mother had taught in Ontario before she was married. Women teachers used to be expected to quit their jobs when they got married, but the war had changed things. Men teachers had enlisted; women had been needed to take their places.

"Your mother will need your cooperation both at school and at home," Father said, "because I have to go away and find work. I'll be leaving for Vancouver."

Grace's jaw dropped. "You're leaving?"

"I'm not deserting the family, Grace, but I have to find work of some kind. Your mother won't earn enough to support the family."

Tears sprang to her eyes. "I don't want you to go."

He sighed. "Grace, ever since you were little you've seen me go away on tours and conferences, and I've always come home. Home is where the heart is, and my heart is always with your mother and you children."

But this is different, Grace thought. Those trips before were part of your work. Now you have no work. What will you do?

"We'll miss you," she whispered.

"I'll miss you too. The good part of serving this pastoral charge was being at home and part of our family's daily life. I want to stay connected with you little shavers, and you can do something to help me."

He got up, reached to the top shelf, and took down a big cloth-bound book with blank, blue-lined pages. Grace stared at it.

"I'd like you to keep a family journal for me. You and the other children can write about what you're doing. Poems and fiction are welcome, too. Then when I come home I can catch up on what interests you, and see how your writing improves."

Grace took the ledger, blinking back tears.

"Bruce and the Kid can't write," she said in a choked voice.

"Then write for them. Ask they what they'd like to say, and put it down. By the way, I wish you'd stop calling Howard 'the Kid'. It makes me think of outlaws in the wild west, like 'Billy the Kid' and 'The Sundance Kid'. We don't want him to become a gun-slinger, do we?"

She couldn't help but laugh, for Howard was just a toddler.

"A family journal is a good idea," she said. "Ralph is beginning to write, and he and Bruce like to draw and the Kid, er, Howard, scribbles."

"All right then. You're in charge of this anthology, and you may give it a name."

"We'll call it *Father's Book*."

He smiled and patted her head.

CHAPTER TWO

END OF APRIL, 1919

"It's so beautiful here! I love it here in the woods."

Kathy smiled as Grace flung her arms wide as if to embrace the towering trees with thick straight trunks that seemed to taper to infinity in the clouds. Sunshine peeped through the layers of leaves and needles, dappling the ferny forest floor. Everything was so green. Mother said her ancestors had come from Ireland, the emerald isle, but surely nothing could be greener than this British Columbia forest.

As Grace said all this, Kathy swished her hair back from her face and laughed.

"Kid, you sound like someone who has been let out of the house for the first time. There must have been trees in Manitoba. I know there's no ocean near Winnipeg, but there must be lakes."

Grace laughed too. "Of course there are. In the summers we used to go to a lakeshore cottage.

Winnipeg has big parks and it's a bustling city. But this forest is so lush, and these mossy logs on the forest floor look like a picture from a book of fairy tales."

"A logging company cut in this area years ago and left them behind."

Grace inhaled the freshness of ferns and firs, blended with cherry blossoms. Back in the 1880s, the first settlers here at the Landing had planted fruit trees, and ever since, farmers had been shipping fruit by steamboat to the Vancouver market. Now many people, including her friend Anna's family, grew vegetables on the flat land above the waterfront. Father admired the Finnish families' community spirit; they had built two meeting halls and were planning a co-op store. Other residents of the Landing were of English background, from the eastern Canadian provinces and from Britain.

"I envy you for having lived in a big city like Winnipeg," Kathy remarked. "I want to live in a city someday. Is it like Vancouver?"

"Well, both are busy and full of people from all over, but Vancouver is a seaport and Winnipeg is a railway centre. Father says Winnipeg is Canada's Chicago."

She paused, wondering what details about Winnipeg would interest Kathy.

"In the north end, some of the newcomers lived in shacks, just one room with a lean-to. Father encouraged them to come to the Mission that he was running, where there was a swimming pool, a kindergarten and lots of interesting programs. There were variety shows there each week, and people sang in their native languages. Some of the songs were sad."

Kathy looked interested. "You mean they were songs in a minor key?"

Grace nodded. "Yes, but sometimes the singers looked sad, as if missing their homes far away."

Both girls fell silent. Then Grace sprang up.

"We should get busy and gather some moss for that vivarium," she said, opening the burlap sack they had brought with them.

One of Kathy's brothers was making a miniature habitat of creepy crawly creatures as his science project, but he had a bad cold, so the girls had offered to gather the moss for him. Grace knelt and flicked away a bug from her hand. The moss was a little world of insect life, the tufts like tiny trees.

Although he was a very busy man, Kathy's dad had found time to put a sliding pane of glass into the top of a wooden box for his son's vivarium. Dr. Fred, as he was known, healed the sick in the coastal communities from Half Moon Bay to Port Mellon, often travelling by boat. Locally, he made his rounds on Paddy the horse. He'd designed and built Stonehurst, the twenty room house where he and his wife, Alice, were raising their six children. Somehow, he made time to help with school projects, play catch, and go on cook-outs on the beach, where he fried ocean perch over a campfire.

When Grace's family had needed a place to stay, he and Aunt Alice had offered them the upstairs of Stonehurst without hesitation. "The more, the merrier," he'd said. Grace and her brothers and sisters called Fred and Alice "Uncle" and "Aunt", honourary titles, and truly they seemed like kindly relatives.

Though children sometimes got on Father's nerves, kids didn't seem to bother Uncle Fred. Ralph, Grace's seven year old brother, tagged around after him, always eager to help him find driftwood for their beach fires. Ralph loved Dr. Fred's tales about life in the far north, travelling by dogsled and snowshoe to make house calls. One night, when Grace had listened to Ralph's prayers, he'd confided that when he grew up he was going to be a doctor like Uncle Fred.

Grace sighed. She wished their own father were at home more, to take them on walks and teach them things. Though he could be strict, and sometimes boring, his absences left a big gap in their life.

"This should be enough moss." Kathy placed a last handful of moss in the sack and wiped her hands on the burlap outside.

"I'll carry it if you like."

"O.K. I'll take it when you get tired."

They made their way down the path and out into the clearing at the top of the hill, where there was fine view of the "The Landing." The stores, houses and churches along Marine Drive looked like the toy village she'd seen years earlier in a Winnipeg department store window. She spotted Stonehurst, the Methodist Church and the manse, even the "Dragon Castle" tree. The sun sparkled on the water, with fishing boats providing dots of colour. The people on the town wharf where the Union Steamships docked were small as Thumbelina. Today the waves lapped gently but sometimes they were wild and white-capped.

In the early morning mist the bay blended with mountains and sky. The snow-topped peaks of the coastal mountains always seemed magical to Grace because they changed colour throughout the day. At sunrise they were golden. At the end of the day the sunset turned them rosy pink. During the day they were ever-changing shades of green and gray.

Kathy noticed Grace's gaze. "You really like the mountains," she remarked.

"From the first moment I saw them, they made me feel safe," Grace replied. "They're like a wall protecting our perfect life here from the rest of the world."

Kathy looked quizzically at Grace.

"I'm glad you like it here, but do you really think it's perfect?" she asked.

Grace turned pink. She shook her head.

"I'd like to think we're sheltered from the world's troubles, but I know some of them have reached us."

"Like the Spanish influenza," Kathy remarked.

Grace nodded. The children had been ill with it, and Ralph had almost died.

"Well, the war is finally over, and I'm thankful," she told Kathy. "It really set people against each other here. But the Armistice Day celebration last November, with the big bonfire on the beach was great, because the whole community came together. I'm hoping bad feelings will heal."

"People say it was the war to end all wars," Kathy remarked, "but my dad isn't so sure about that. And I don't think feelings will heal right away. Think of Tommy Smith."

Grace's forehead wrinkled. She felt badly about Tommy. He was a school mate, though not exactly a chum these days, because he was angry all the time. Tommy's father and uncle had volunteered in 1914 as part of the Canadian Expeditionary Force, and two years later his father was killed in battle. Tommy's Uncle Walt had survived and returned to the Landing, but people said he wasn't well, and he didn't go out of the house much.

Grace then noticed that Kathy's pink hair ribbon had come loose and that she was in danger of losing it.

"Let me tie your bow," she said. Kathy bent down and Grace swept her light brown hair away from her face, retying the satin ribbon firmly. Her own dark brown hair was in a braid down her back.

"One of these days I'm getting my hair bobbed," she said.

"I'm not sure I'm ready to lose my long hair," Kathy replied. "I mentioned to Dad the other night that short hair is the latest fashion for women and he said that of all the changes the war has brought, that's the least important one."

Grace sometimes got tired of discussing world events.

"Let's race back to the house," she suggested. "First to get to the front porch wins."

"Sure!" said Kathy. "On your mark. Get set. Go!"

The burlap bag of moss bounced against Grace's legs as she ran. Kathy, who was in the lead, was a blur of black stockings, with her hair streaming out behind her. Grace's braid thumped between her shoulder blades. Down the trail they galloped. They tore through the back yard and around the house, almost upsetting Dr. Fred in his camp chair as they made for the porch. Kathy won, but just by a nose.

Dr. Fred looked up from his paper.

"Hey, you two fillies. Are you practising for the derby?"

The girls sank onto the grass to catch their breath. On the front veranda were Grace's brothers: ten year old Charles, seven year old Ralph, and five year old Bruce, along with Kath's brothers and little sister. From the downstairs window floated the lively tune, *Camp Town Races*. Aunt Alice tried to find few minutes every day to practise the organ. As the tune ended, Grace heard a child's howl and a soft voice saying, "There, there now."

She looked up and saw her twelve year old sister, Belva, on the second storey balcony with young Howard in her arms. He buried his face in her collar and the two of them withdrew.

"Have a seat, young ladies, and hear the latest news." Uncle Fred tapped his finger on an article in his folded newspaper. "Workers in Canada are going to rise up and demand their fair share of the fruits of their labour like they've done in Russia. They're sick and tired of wages that aren't keeping up with the cost of living and they're not going to put up with them any more. They're going to strike."

His eyes twinkled as he looked at Grace. He and her father had argued about Russia many times.

"A strike isn't the same as a revolution," Grace said calmly, "and Canada isn't like Russia was under the Czar. We don't need to overthrow the government to get better wages and working conditions."

Uncle Fred smiled. "Grace, you're a chip off the old block. You sound just like your Pa. Here, have my paper. Your mother may want to read it if she has time. According to what I read, your old home town of Winnipeg is a bubbling volcano about to erupt. Apparently the metal and building trade unions are fed up with employers who won't pay them a living wage. What do you hear about that?"

"Not much," Grace said. "Our relatives in Winnipeg haven't mentioned much about it in their letters, and Father hasn't been back there since we left in 1917."

"Grace!"

Grace looked up. Mother was waving from the upstairs veranda.

"Hello, Fred." She leaned over the rail, smiling. "Grace, dear, I need your help."

"Excuse me. I'll see you all later."

"The queen of your household needs assistance," joked Uncle Fred, "and you, the crown princess, must come to her aid."

"Uncle Fred, you know there's hardly any royalty around any more," Grace said with a smile. "No more Russian royal family, no more Kaiser Wilhelm on the German throne. So how can I be a crown princess?"

"Pardon me," said the doctor. "*Comrade* Grace, your mother needs you."

Laughing, Grace ran up the outside flight of stairs to the second storey, to see what Mother wanted.

CHAPTER THREE

Upstairs she found Howard cranky after his nap. Belva was eager to hand him over to her and to help Mother cook dinner.

"Grace, could you take him into your room and read to him?" Mother asked.

"Sure." She took her little brother by the hand.

"And tomorrow, my dear, I'm going to need your help. I have to go in early to prepare work for the Entrance class so you'll have to take the two little boys to Mrs. Erola's house."

Mrs. Erola was the babysitter/housekeeper who came in on weekdays.

"Why isn't she coming here?"

"She and her husband are sorting and packing cherries to send to Vancouver. If she's at home, she can work at that while the little boys nap."

"All right," said Grace. "I'll drop them off."

Bruce, the second youngest, grabbed Grace's other hand and said he knew where their favourite book was.

If Mother was unavailable, the younger children knew that Grace was the person to go to with a scratched knee, wounded feelings, or a tough arithmetic problem. When Mother had to stay late at school to meet with the other teachers and plan lessons, Grace always went straight home and took over from Mrs. Erola.

Grace, too, was the one who reminded the others of their assigned tasks on the roster that Mother had tacked to the kitchen wall. All the children had to do their part to keep the home running smoothly. There were no "girls' jobs" and "boys' jobs". Grace and Belva took their turns keeping the woodbox full, cleaning out the ashes and taking the garbage to the compost heap, while Charles, and to a lesser extent, Ralph, took turns making beds, doing dishes and folding laundry. Belva liked cooking and was always eager to trade tasks to have the opportunity. Bruce and Howard were supposed to pick up their toys from underfoot when they were finished playing with them.

That night Grace and Belva did the dishes while Mother got busy with some mending. Grace went to bed early and fell asleep immediately. In the early morning, before it was light, she woke briefly. Someone was padding around in the kitchen, probably Mother, up with one of the younger children. She rolled over and fell asleep.

Next morning, Belva had already gotten up when Grace rose. She hurried into her clothes and went to the kitchen, where the other children, except for Charles, were having breakfast. Mother, dressed for school, was pouring milk. The satchel containing her books and papers was by the door.

"I have to run," Mother said. "Grace, wake Charles up, and wipe off your little brothers' faces before you take them to Mrs. Erola's."

"All rightie." Grace went to get a washcloth, then served herself some porridge. She would give Charles ten more minutes. The others finished their meal and Grace went in to check on Charles. He was flat on his back in bed. In the light of the window she saw crimson dots all over his face, neck, hands and arms. He had some kind of rash.

"I feel sick." He moaned.

Grace's stomach churned. Was it measles? Scarlet fever? Surely not the deadly influenza again, that had laid them all low several months earlier. She asked him to stick out his tongue. It wasn't coated.

"Stay in bed. I'll get you an aspirin and some water. I'll ask Aunt Alice to come up and look in on you this morning."

"Thanks," he murmured. "I just need rest."

"I have to run."

The little boys, with their short legs, took a long time to get to the Erolas' and Grace had to run to get to school by nine o'clock.

"What happened to you?" whispered Kathy, across the aisle.

Grace whispered an explanation. "I just hope we don't all come down with something. Is your dad in town today?"

"I think he's going to Sechelt this morning."

"I was going to ask your mother to look in on Charles but I forgot."

"We'll check on him at noon hour," Kathy said.

As soon as the noon bell rang, Grace and Kathy were out of school like a shot. They tore down the hill to the house, raced panting up the outside staircase to the second storey apartment, and, puffing, opened the door.

There was Charles, fully dressed at the kitchen table, the remains of a sandwich on a plate beside him. He was cleaning his most prized possession, his .22 calibre rifle.

"You shouldn't be up. You'll get chilled!" Grace exclaimed. "Here, let me feel your forehead."

His forehead wasn't hot. In the noon light, she noticed that the spots on his face didn't rise above the skin's surface. Some of them looked blurry. She licked her hand, touched his forehead again, and her touch made a red smear.

"This isn't a rash, this is watercolour paint!" she cried. Kathy wet her hand and touched his cheek, and the red dots came off in on her hand too.

"Oh, Charles you're such a fraud!" roared Grace. "You got up in the middle of the night and painted your face!"

Kathy giggled. Grace didn't know whether to stay angry, or laugh.

"You gave me a terrible fright," she said.

"Aw, Grace, I didn't feel like going in to class this morning," he said. "I needed some time to myself. You have to admit I'm a good painter. I'm like that French fellow Mother told us about – Seurat – who paints his canvases in little dots of paint. A *pointillist*, that's the word. I'm a *pointillist*."

"That's not the word I'd use," Grace said sternly. "Wash yourself right now and get ready for school. Otherwise, I'm going to tell Mother about your mysterious rash and she'll be so disappointed in you."

He sighed and went to wash his face. Grace broke into a smile. Still, what with Charles's prank, and rumours of labour unrest from across the mountains, she felt edgy all afternoon. Then, after school, when she went for the mail and found a letter from Father, her heart lightened. Maybe he was coming home!

CHAPTER FOUR

Over their evening meal, Mother read the children the letter from Father, except for a bit at the end that was just for her. The good news was that he was coming home, on Saturday, and leaving early Monday morning.

"I want him to be able to relax in a clean, orderly home," Mother said. "I need your help in tidying this apartment from one end to the other."

Over the next few days, they did. They hung blankets on the upstairs veranda to air, and took the rugs out on the lawn to beat the dust out of them. Mother bought new oil cloth for the table but over-estimated the amount required, so the left-over piece was put in the hall closet for when it might be needed.

On Friday afternoon after school, Grace was alone in the apartment except for Howard, who was napping.

"The poor kid must be exhausted," she thought, "if he can sleep through the noise." Belva, Ralph, and the younger children in Kathy's family were on the lawn playing tag. Kathy was practising on her mother's parlour organ, her tunes wafting up from below.

Grace peeled potatoes for supper and put them in water. Then she swept and scrubbed the kitchen floor. After that, she went out to reel in the clothes on the line. She wanted everything shipshape before Mother came home.

As she put the clean garments in a basket, she gazed at the snow-capped mountains across Howe Sound. She hoped Father wasn't coming home to announce another move. Though she sometimes longed to see her relatives in Winnipeg, she didn't miss the snow and extreme cold that gave that city the nickname "Winterpeg." Here on the Sunshine Coast there was winter rain but seldom snow that stayed. Here, you could go barefoot almost all year round.

She hoped Father would be relaxed when he got home. Both her parents had been awfully sad on moving from Winnipeg early in 1917. They hated leaving Grandmother behind, especially as Grandfather had died just a few months before they left. Worse, when they left, few of their friends came to say goodbye. Mother told Grace that people were probably reluctant to be seen with anyone who questioned Canada's involvement in the Great War.

For the children, the move west had been a glorious adventure. Travelling on a train, going through the mountains, heading toward the Pacific Ocean – what could be more exciting? And they'd ended up here in this jewel of a town, and now were at Stonehurst, with wonderful friends. Though her parents and Fred and

Alice sometimes disagreed about politics and world events, they never got tired of talking to each other.

Folding clothes, she thought of the ongoing discussion between her father and Uncle Fred about events in Russia.

Back in 1917 – it was now late April, 1919 – the czar and his wealthy, privileged supporters were overthrown in the name of the people, and Russia had dropped out of the war. A moderate party of the left formed a new government, but in late 1917 the Bolsheviks, the more extreme leftist party, took over power. Two revolutions had occurred in one year. Now a civil war was being fought, with the Bolsheviks and their supporters on one side and their opponents on the other. The Bolsheviks, who now called themselves "Communists", seemed to be losing, according to the newspaper reports.

Uncle Fred had been very excited by the 1917 revolutions in Russia, and, in conversations with her parents, said he wished everyday people everywhere, including Canada, would overthrow their oppressors. Listening in on this conversation, Grace had wondered: Was he serious, or just playing for effect?

Father had disagreed with him.

"Canada is a different situation entirely," he'd insisted. "Here, we don't need a revolution because we've had elected governments for years. What Canadians must do is elect Members of Parliament who care about the needs of everyday working people. Then they'll pass laws to make the country fair and free."

Now that Father was coming home, Grace expected that he and Uncle Fred would pick up their discussion where they'd left off.

Smoothing the wrinkles in one of Charles's shirts, she remembered an incident in Winnipeg when she was little. She was walking along the wooden sidewalk hand in hand with Father, when some tough older boys hassled them.

They pointed at Father. "Hey, Czar Nicholas!" one called. Another said, "Hey, King George."

Grace was alarmed and confused. Back home, Father and Mother had laughed over the incident and explained to her why they'd called Father these names.

Some newcomers to Canada, living in the crowded north end of Winnipeg, had come from parts of Europe where people were scared of the czar, who had absolute powers of life and death over his people. The king of England and the late czar of Russia had been look-alike first cousins, and Father, a neatly-dressed slender man with a short beard, must have reminded these youths of these rulers in their old countries. Later, comparing pictures of the king, the czar and Father, Grace didn't see much resemblance. Father wasn't stern like them, not when he smiled. She noticed that later on, the youths who had shouted at Father showed up to use the gym in the Stella Avenue Mission which Father ran, so she guessed they'd gotten over their suspicions.

Now Grace smoothed the white middy blouses that she and Belva wore. These garments made them look as if they were in the Navy – if there were such a thing as a girl sailor! One blouse had a button missing. She located the button box and was poising the button on her needle when feet came pounding up the stairs.

Charles burst into the room, shirtless, and went to the ice box for milk. His hair was slicked down and there were beads of water on his back.

"Did you take the little ones swimming?" she asked.

"No." He had a milk moustache on his upper lip. "I went with some other guys."

Grace made a face in envy. She loved swimming.

"Put on a shirt and help me fold these clothes," Grace ordered.

"Ja-vol!" Charles brought his heels together and raised his hand in a salute.

"Don't do that. Father would hate it."

"You're like a Prussian officer, Grace, the way you boss us kids around."

Grace grinned. "You're always up to something, Charles, so I have to be tough."

He chuckled. She held out the sheet to him.

"This is one odd-looking sheet," he remarked, as he brought his corners up to hers.

The freshly-laundered sheet was covered with printing in ink that wouldn't come off. As Grace and he brought their sheet corners together again, she read: "value of their labour" and "people before profits". There were also numbers – statistics about the numbers of men killed and wounded at one stage of the war. Father had used this sheet and others to write important facts on when giving talks at the local community halls last year, before he went to Vancouver. When he spoke in schools he always had a blackboard, but not in the halls, so he wrote out the main points on the sheets beforehand, then nailed them to the wall so people could see and remember. Now that Father was a stevedore, Mother had reclaimed the sheets and was using them on the beds again, saying that they were perfectly good and that they couldn't afford new ones.

"I agree, they're strange," Grace now told Charles. "I'm glad our clothesline is at the back of the house facing the woods so people don't see them. But we're used to sleeping between statistics. And some families don't have any sheets at all."

She picked up another sheet, but Charles backed away.

"I can't fold," he said. "I'm all thumbs. Besides, I have to do my story for Father's Book. It's about tugboats and I know he'll like it if I get it finished. What are you going to show him?"

"My French test. I got an A plus."

"You always do."

He disappeared into the boys' room to change his clothes as Grace sewed on the button. On returning, he flopped onto a chair and studied her.

"Are you looking forward to having Father home?" he asked.

"Of course. Aren't you?"

He shrugged. "Yes, but I hope he doesn't try to smarten us up too much."

She laughed. "I know what you mean. He likes to instruct."

A couple of times in the recent past when Father came home, Grace had asked him to help her with a schoolwork problem. He made sure she knew the background and all aspects of the question, an explanation that seemed to go on forever. Grace couldn't help but fidget, watch the clock and wish she hadn't asked.

When he was last home, she hadn't been able to find her good black stockings and had asked Mother where they were.

"In the drawer," Mother had said.

"No they're not. I can't find them."

With a sigh, Father had told her to look again. Then he'd come into the bedroom she shared with Belva, pulled open the top dresser drawer, and made her straighten out the contents, which included her missing stockings.

"*A place for everything and everything in its place,*" he'd declared.

Was that a Bible verse? Grace didn't ask. She admired Father for being neat and well-organized, but she was more like Mother, who was awfully busy and put things away in haphazard fashion.

"Unloading shipments on the docks doesn't give Father much opportunity to teach," she told Charles.

"If he sermonized at them, those big stevedores would pop him one."

Grace gasped. "Charles, what a thing to say!"

He shrugged. "They're big tough men who don't take guff from anyone."

Grace wondered again how a slight, skinny man like Father was able to do the heavy lifting that these burly dock workers did.

"Tell me again what about that time he took you to the dockyards," she said.

"Well, it was a bit scary," Charles began. "It was raining that night and we had to watch our step because those high wooden wharves are slippery when wet. They were lit by lights on poles. We made our way to where a gigantic crane was being used to lift a net-load of boxes and bundles out of the hold of a big ship. The man directing the crane would shout at the workers every now and then, and every time he did it I would jump. The big bundle of boxes in the net hit the dock with a thud, and that really made the crane guy mad, because one of the wooden boxes burst open. Tea spilled out all over."

"Did they shovel it into the sea?"

"No," said Charles "They shovelled it back into the wooden crate, and that crate went to the buyer, and the tea ended up in somebody's teapot. The men couldn't stop to worry about that, though; they had to keep working. Some of them were moving the shipment on wheeled carts to the warehouses. Several of them called out hello. One said: *Hey, James, is that your boy?* and Father said, *Yes, this is my son, Charles.*"

Charles's voice faltered, and his face crumpled up as if he were going to cry.

"He's proud of you, Charles," said Grace. "I know you miss him."

"The men at the docks like Father and he likes them. He gets awful tired from the work, though."

"He'll want to rest when he gets home and we'll have to try to keep Howard quiet. You know how Howard likes to get into Mother and Father's bed at night? Maybe you could take him in yours, Charles, so our parents won't be crowded."

Charles pulled a face. "The Kid could bunk with you and Belva."

As if they had called his name, the door opened and in came their three year old brother, pint-sized but a force of nature. Close on his heels was Belva, looking flustered, and last of all came Mother, carrying her shopping basket over her arm, looking calm and serene. Grace relaxed. Now that Mother was home, everything would fall into place. Soon they would be enjoying a good supper; then she would oversee the last of the housecleaning and baking that needed doing before Father's return.

"I want a cookie!" the Kid announced.

Belva wiped her sweaty forehead on her sleeve.

"Those are for when Father comes home. I don't want them all eaten before he gets here."

"But I want one!"

Mother bent down and threw her arms around the Kid.

"Give me a kiss, you big boy!" she said. "Howard, a cookie now will spoil your supper. You'll have one later for dessert. If you're truly hungry, Belva will get you a slice of bread and butter."

Howard made a face and shook his head.

"Belva, get a washcloth and wipe off his hands and face. Help Ralph and Bruce wash up, too," she added, as the two little boys came running in. "Charles, put those blankets in the bedrooms and then set the table. And Grace, put the laundry basket in my bedroom and then start peeling some potatoes."

"They're done." Grace picked up the wicker basket.

"Wonderful!" Mother exclaimed.

Getting a meal together was usually hectic. Sometimes Belva took charge and cleared everyone out of the kitchen. Mother praised Belva's cooking but made sure that meal preparation didn't fall to her alone, because she needed time to study and have fun. Tonight, Belva began frying halibut in butter with a sprinkling of dill, while Mother opened a sealer of tomato preserves. As Charles put out plates and cutlery, Ralph sat on the kitchen floor with a piece of lined paper propped on a thick dictionary. He had a lead pencil in his hand and was writing a story to show Father. Bruce, who was planning to draw something, was looking over Ralph's shoulder. Howard was there too, with the cat in his arms.

Then a piercing scream cut the air. Mother put the sealer down with a thud and wheeled to see what was the matter. Ralph was howling. The cat, in Howard's arms, had been hanging above Ralph, and had reached out for support and dug her claws into his neck.

Mother fell to her knees to look at the scratch, as Ralph sobbed.

"It's not that bad," she told him. "Someone get the iodine."

"No, that stings!"

Grace wet a rag and gave it to her mother to wipe the thin line of blood. The scratch didn't look deep; the insult was worse than the injury. Belva noticed that the potatoes were about to boil over, and lifted the pot from the stove.

Mother turned to the Kid, who had released the cat and was looking on with interest.

"Howard, why did you let the cat scratch your brother?" she asked.

"She wanted to see what he was drawing."

Ralph wiped his eyes on his fists and began to laugh.

"Kids!" thought Grace. When she grew up she wasn't having any!

"What's going on?" inquired a deep voice. All eyes turned to the doorway.

CHAPTER FIVE

"It's Father!" Charles exclaimed.

Ralph forgot his scratch and bounded toward the slight man in the doorway.

Mother, too, rushed over and hugged Father.

"We thought you were coming tomorrow," she cried.

Then she gathered Howard into her arms because he always acted as if Father were a stranger.

"I thought I'd come early and surprise you. How are all my little shavers?" Father hugged each of the children in turn as they clustered around him. Belva abandoned the fish and rushed to embrace him.

"We missed you!" she exclaimed.

He surprised us and caught us in a mess, as usual, Grace thought. Seeing that the fish was done, she lifted the pan off the heat. Then, as she went over to greet her father, her annoyance vanished as she noticed how dusty and worn he looked.

"I got a ride in a friend's motor boat," he said. "When I was coming up the road I heard a scream. What's wrong?"

"Nothing. Family life. A cat scratch." Mother helped him off with his coat. "Come and take your place at the head of the table."

"What's in the bag?" asked Bruce, pointing to the burlap sack that Father had set down with his small valise at the door.

"I'll show you later." Father pulled out his chair and sat down. Mother deposited Howard on his lap.

"Do you have a kiss for a tired old longshoreman?" Father asked him, and the little boy got over being shy and planted a kiss on his cheek.

"It's good to be home," Father declared. "I have so much to tell you."

"And we have things to tell you too," said Ralph.

As the others took their places, Grace helped her mother serve, then slid onto a chair. Father bowed his head to give thanks.

"We are thankful for these and all the good things of life," he said. "We know they come to us through the efforts of our brothers and sisters the world over. What we desire for ourselves we wish for all. To this end, may we take our share in the world's work and the world's struggles."

"Amen!" said the Kid, loudly. Everybody smiled and echoed "Amen."

"It's good to have you home, James," said Mother, passing him the fish platter. "We've missed you, haven't we, children?"

There was a chorus of "Yes."

"Tell us your news," Mother urged.

"Oh, that can wait. I want to hear what all of you have been doing."

Everyone wanted to talk first, but Mother made them go in turn, starting with the youngest. Ralph and Bruce wanted to sing "*Tipperary*" for Father but Mother said, "Not at the table." Charles said he was writing an essay on tugboats for the family annual scrapbook but hadn't finished it yet.

"Good," said Father. "I'm glad you're showing an interest in the practical sciences. When you're ready for high school, son, we'll find a good technical school for you. One thing I've learned from being tossed into the world of casual manual labour is that it's good to have a trade."

"Yes, sir." Charles's forelock of dark brown hair fell into his eyes and he brushed it back. "I'm also reading *The Adventures of Robin Hood and his Merry Men.* You'd like it, Father, because Robin robbed from the rich to give to the poor."

"I've read it, Charles It's a great story that shows what happens when the government is out of touch with the people. But we don't live in the Middle Ages. This is the twentieth century and we don't want to rob anybody, do we?"

"We want the country run in such a way that everyone gets a fair share of the good things in life," said Grace.

"That's right." Father turned to Mother. "That brings me to my news. Will Ivens in Winnipeg has asked me to make a speaking trip across the western provinces. I'm to talk to workers' organizations about building a free and fair society now that the war is over."

Mother's face lit up.

"You'll be good at that," she said promptly, "and I'm delighted for you. But you'll be away from home for long periods of time, won't you?"

Father looked sad. "Yes, but I'll write, and send money, and whenever I'm in Vancouver I'll come home."

There was silence all around the table.

"That reminds me, Lucy," Father added. "Do you have any sheets that I could use on my speaking tour?"

Mother frowned. "I think there's one."

"Why do you write on sheets, Father?" piped up Bruce. He was just five and had always been home in bed, back when Father used to give talks at the Finnish Hall and the Socialist Hall here at the Landing.

"So people can see what I'm saying as well as hear it," Father said. "Having the main words and figures on a blackboard or poster helps the audience understand and remember."

The Kid squirmed around on Father's lap and grabbed his beard.

"Father, don't go away again," he said.

Father smiled.

"I have to," he said, "but you children will be in my thoughts all the time I'm away. Now, let's not talk about me. I'd rather hear from you. Belva, what have you been doing since I was home last?"

Belva blushed at being singled out.

"Studying for the entrance, and going swimming, and hemming my new skirt."

"Good for you. And Grace? Any new poems to show me?"

Grace shook her head. She didn't like showing Father her poetry because he always spotted little mistakes, like lines that didn't quite scan and rhyme that wasn't exact.

"No," she said. "But I have an idea. Since we're here at the table, let's play the question and answer game about who provided our supper."

"All right." Father looked pleased that she remembered it. "Do you little boys remember it?"

Ralph, Bruce and the Kid shook their heads. Even Charles, who was ten, looked doubtful.

"I'll begin," said Grace. "O.K. Who set our dinner table?"

"That's easy," said Charles "I did."

"Yes, you did," said Grace, "but who provided the table cloth?"

Charles looked stumped. "Mother? Or maybe our grandmother in Ontario?" he guessed.

"That's right," said Mother, smiling. "But where did she get it?"

Belva spoke up. "She had it in her cedar chest. Long ago it came from Ireland."

Father nodded. "Right you are. It's made of linen. Do you know where linen comes from?"

Grace knew, but she glanced down at the table cloth, stained and fraying after fifteen years of use. She knew that linen was made from the flax plant, and thought that Charles did too. This time, she would keep quiet and give him his chance to shine. Sometimes Father got cross with Charles because he was boisterous and mischievous.

"Flax," Charles said. "It's a plant."

"It certainly is. Farmers grow it, and weavers weave the fibre into cloth, so we can say that farmers and weavers helped us set our supper table. And who gave us our plates?

"Charles did," said little Bruce.

Father smiled. "Charles put them on the table, but where did the plates come from?"

Ralph, who had cleared his plate, turned it over and read, on the bottom, "Great Britain."

Then Father explained that in a part of faraway England called the Black Country, people made pottery, first shaping it from clay, then glazing it and baking it in a kiln. The little boys stared at the very plain dinnerware as if seeing it for the first time.

"How did it get here?" asked Bruce.

"In barrels packed with straw on a big ship that came across the ocean," said Mother. "Your father unloads barrels like that."

"A great many workers all over the world helped make our supper possible," Father remarked.

Ralph looked puzzled.

"Mother and the girls made the food," he said. "Mother bought fish and Belva fried it, and Grace peeled the potatoes and Belva had already baked the cookies."

"We *prepared* the food," Mother agreed, "but let's think of where it came from."

Soon the younger children were talking about fishermen, farmers, railway workers, millers, bakers, butchers, milkmen and grocers.

"So you see," said Mother, "When I serve dinner every day I'm being helped by hardworking people all over the world."

"And, without their help, we wouldn't have be having a good dinner like this one," Father added. "Now, did someone mention cookies?"

CHAPTER SIX

"Have there been any more spills of tea on the docks?" Charles asked Father that evening. The family had gathered in the small living room, the little children in their nightshirts.

"No, but I saw a man narrowly escape from a runaway barrel," Father said. "It would have injured him if it had struck him, but it didn't."

Grace, in a corner, saw her mother's apprehensive look. She worries about him all the time, she thought.

"Dock workers need to have their wits about them at all times," Father continued. "Did I ever tell you about my first days of looking for work in Vancouver?"

The children shook their heads. If he had, they wanted to hear about it again.

"When you first went to Vancouver with Uncle Fred to look for work, I thought you'd become a teacher in a school," Charles remarked.

Father nodded. "That was my first thought too, but the only school that needed a teacher was on the western coast of Vancouver Island. The pay was low and it would have been hard to get home on the weekends. Then Fred suggested that I go to see Mr. Winch of the Longshoremen's Union and the Trades and Labour Council, and that was an inspired idea. Mr. Winch was interested in my situation and thought I should do some writing and public speaking while earning a living moving freight to and from the carts and sheds. Teaching school, you're chained to the job; you can't take a day off to write an article or attend a meeting or you'd get fired. Working on the docks, if I take time off to come and see all of you, I can go back and still have the opportunity to earn."

"Explain to them how the hiring is done," Mother prompted.

"Well, you go to the hiring hall. The Longshoremen's Hall is in an old church near the waterfront. We sit in the auditorium reading or playing cards, or stand outside. As the steamboats come in, gangs of men are sent for, but you have to wait your turn. Sometimes when there isn't enough work only eight or ten men are called and a hundred or so are left waiting in the rain. On my first day, I and another fellow were sent to the Great Northern freight sheds, to unload a big shipment of rubber, in boxes weighing 150 to 200 pounds. I realized I should have worn work gloves to protect my hands. I slipped around the corner and bought a pair and then got down to work. That first day was exhausting. Luckily the boss didn't make us rush."

"I'd like to visit the docks," Ralph piped up.

"Me too," said Bruce. "I'd like to see the big crane and all the men."

"It sounds hard but you seem to like working there," Grace remarked.

Father nodded. "I do. I've made a lot of friends and heard a lot of people's stories. Most have problems far worse than ours."

Father was happy to be in a union, joining with other workers to push for better pay and working conditions. On Sunday nights he sometimes spoke at the labour outreach meetings at a theatre downtown. He also wrote for the union paper.

"What do you write?" asked Ralph.

Father smiled. "*Not* inspirational essays about the beauty and satisfaction of work. Grinding physical labour day after day isn't inspiring. You get through your shift and all you want to do is eat and go to bed."

"Are you going on strike?" asked Charles.

"Not that I've heard of," Father said.

"Uncle Fred says there were a lot of strikes all over Canada last year," Grace chipped in, "and there will be more and more, leading to a revolution like in Russia."

Father raised his eyebrows. "I don't think so. Our federal government demanded an awful lot from working people during the war, and it has encouraged the greedy while neglecting the needy, but I believe we can bring change in this country by peaceful means."

"Is Uncle Fred bad?" asked five year old Bruce.

Father laughed. "Absolutely not! Fred is brilliant, and a humanitarian. We have a slight difference of opinion on politics, that's all."

"Dr. Fred heals the sick," added Mother. "He and Aunt Alice are our best friends. They were kind enough to put a roof over our heads. He's a good neighbour to everyone."

"Thinking of kind friends," said Father, "the Winch family sent us some good used clothing that their boy, Harry, has outgrown. Grace, would you fetch that bag at the door?"

"New clothes!" Grace sprang up eagerly. Then, as she brought the sack over to the centre of their circle, she realized she was excited for nothing. Harry was a boy, so obviously the clothes would be for her brothers, with nothing for her and Belva.

Father reached into the bag and pulled out the object that was making it so bulky – a shiny new tin breadbox, with pictures of bread on the lid and sides. It wasn't scratched up like their old one. He handed it to Mother.

Mother smiled. "A token of your affection! Thank you."

Father turned red. "I was just being practical."

"And I'm just teasing. It's very nice," Mother insisted. "We've had the other one since we were married and it has a lot of scratches and dents."

She handed it to Belva.

"Take it to the kitchen, please, my dear, and put the bread in it. We'll save the old box. It may come in handy for something."

Then Mother reached into the bag and pulled out a blue shirt.

"Charles, isn't this grand!" she exclaimed. "It ought to fit you. Try it on."

The sleeves were slightly long, but Mother said she could shorten them. Most of the clothes fit Charles, and a few items fit Ralph and Bruce. Belva found a wine coloured pull-over sweater and matching tam o'shanter for herself. A little pair of black boots were just the size for Howard. There was nothing for Grace, though. Then, Charles, who was trying on a pair of boots, said they were too big.

"I'd have to stuff the toes with newspaper to make them fit," he said. "Or maybe they'd fit you, Grace. You're older, with bigger feet."

Grace's one pair of shoes, plain and black like these boots, pinched her toes. She'd been planning to go barefoot all summer and get new shoes in fall. But maybe these boots would fit.

"Let me try them."

Charles handed over the boots and she put them on. They fit perfectly.

"Oh, Grace, you're not going to wear boys' boots to school!" murmured Belva.

Grace did a jig in her new footwear.

"They're plain black boots," she told Belva. "No one can tell if they're for a boy or for a girl. You can have my old shoes if you want."

"I'll write to thank the Winch family," said Mother. Then she turned to the children. "Instead of my reading aloud this evening, let's make up a co-operative story. You know the kind, where we all take turns adding a bit."

"I haven't heard one of those stories in a long time." Father shifted the Kid to a more comfortable position on his lap.

Grace loved these group stories. The fun lay in stopping at a key point and having someone take over and bend the tale in whatever direction he or she wanted.

"Grace, you're the eldest, so you go first," her father said.

"Once upon a time," Grace began, "there was a young girl who liked going for walks in the forest. Her name was – Waverly."

She chose that name because of one of her parents' jokes. They had been reading Sir Walter Scott's "Waverly" novels before she was born, and they joked that they had thought of calling her "Winona Waverly" instead of "Winona Grace."

"One day when Waverly was out picking berries, she heard in the distance the faint strains of guitar music, and song. She followed the sound and entered a forest glade and there she found several brightly covered caravans parked in a circle around a campfire. The horses were in a rough corral nearby, and some women were stirring stew in a pot on the fire. A man sat on the doorstep of one of the caravans playing his guitar and singing." She turned to Belva. "Now it's your turn."

Belva took a deep breath.

"A young man came out, took Waverly by the hand and led her to the fire. The women offered her some stew and she accepted it, and took a sip from a brown bottle the boy offered her. Soon she became sleepy, leaned against a tree, and drifted off. When she awoke she was bouncing around in the bed of the wagon and could see the night sky from the tiny window. She was all alone and terrified. She had been kidnapped."

"The plot thickens," Father remarked. "Who wants to pick up the story and carry on with it?"

Ralph was waving his hand.

"At home," he began, with enthusiasm, "Waverly's family wondered why she didn't come home for supper. They looked everywhere for her and asked all the neighbours, and someone remembered that she had gone to pick berries. One neighbour had a bloodhound, so they let it sniff Waverly's clothes and then, knowing her scent, it took off into the woods. He led them to the place where the gypsies had camped but all that was left was some horse manure and burnt logs."

Bruce looked concerned. The Kid was asleep in Father's arms.

"Who will continue?" Mother asked. "Charles?"

Charles, snickering about the horse manure, took over with enthusiasm.

"Waverly had a brother named Wyatt," he began, "and Wyatt had a rifle, a Winchester. He was well-known as a sure shot and a rodeo rider. He jumped on his horse, the fastest in the village, and went down the road, following the hoof prints and wheel marks left by the caravan. He rode for many a mile, and at nightfall, when he saw a spiral of smoke above the trees, he got off his horse and crept through the bush to the encampment. From behind a clump of trees he saw the gypsies eating, drinking and dancing. Then he saw a young girl, dressed in a red gypsy skirt, sitting on the tongue of one of the wagons, with her head in her hands, crying. It was Waverly. He made his whip-poor-will cry, which she knew so well, and which you could expect to hear in the wild. She lifted her arms so that he could see they were tied with a rope.

"When the moon came out, Wyatt crept silently up to the camp, where the gypsies were lying drunk on the ground. He took his knife and set his sister free. Waverly was so glad he'd come that she made a whimpering noise, and that woke the biggest, toughest gypsy of them all. He got up from where he was sitting, and took out his knife.

"Wyatt aimed the rifle at his head. *My sister leaves with me, or you get a bullet between your eyes*, he said."

Charles broke off, and looked around to see who could follow that. Bruce waved his hand eagerly.

"Wyatt didn't come alone," the five year old began. "He brought his two younger brothers with him and both of them had guns. They told the gypsies to put their hands on their heads and keep them there until they'd counted to one hundred."

Then Ralph chipped in.

"Then the other younger brother grabbed Waverly by the hand and pulled her into the brush and they found the horse and all four of them rode home like greased lightning. When the parents saw that they had rescued Waverly they threw their arms around her, thanked the boys, and then they all had ice cream."

"That was a wonderful story," Mother said. "No, don't clap. Let's not wake the baby. Now, goodnight, and off to bed."

Reluctantly they all headed for their beds, except for Grace and Belva.

"Howard can sleep with us tonight," Grace said in a low voice.

"Thank you girls," said Mother, as Father rose and carried the sleeping three year old into the double bed in the girls' room.

"Goodnight," he said. "And don't dream of gypsies."

Mother came in to kiss the girls goodnight.

"Sleep well," she whispered. "By the way, my darlings, if you'd been the ones who finished that story, you'd have let Waverly figure out a way of escaping, rather than having her be rescued."

CHAPTER SEVEN

The following morning Grace entered the kitchen to find the other children eating breakfast and listening to Mother read softly from *The Railway Children*.

She looked up. "Hello, Grace," she whispered. "Your father needs to sleep in today so we're being very quiet. As soon as everyone has finished eating, we're going for a nature walk in the woods. Have some breakfast. Join us."

A hike? Grace felt weary. She hadn't slept well, and she had a ache in her lower back and a pinching feeling in her lower abdomen. She knew, too, that the Kid would only walk a short distance before he would demand to be carried, and that she, Belva and Mother would have to take turns piggy-backing him. Also, when he was walking, they could never take their eyes off him for fear he'd wander away or sample some woodland berry or bug.

When it was time to go, Grace and Belva helped Bruce and the Kid tie their shoes. Grace decided to leave her legs bare, as the day was warm. It was pleasant to stretch out her toes in the boots that were new to her. Mother gave her a Mason jar of water to carry, and a cookie for each of them tied up in a tea towel. The woods reminded her of the poem *Evangeline* by Henry Wadsworth Longfellow.

"*This is the forest primeval*," she recited, as they walked up the trail.

"*The murmuring pines and the hemlocks/Bearded with moss, and in garments green.*"

"*Indistinct in the twilight/Stand like Druids of Eld, with voices sad and prophetic*," Mother chimed in.

"What's a Druid of Eld?" inquired Charles.

"Of eld means of olden days, of long ago," Mother explained, "and the Druid religion was practised in England during the Stone Age."

"Oh." He sprang in front of Grace and bounded down the trail ahead.

Now that they were outdoors, Grace felt better. The woods were an aviary of calling birds. Charles led the way, singing "*Tipperary*" at the top of his lungs, with Bruce, Ralph and the Kid at his heels. They scared three crows and a blue jay, and let out a screech when a long furry creature, possibly a muskrat or a weasel, streaked across their path and vanished in the underbrush.

Howard turned to Mother and held out his arms to be picked up.

"We all need a rest," she said. "Charles, find a good place for a picnic."

"Here's one," he shouted back.

They met up with him in a cathedral-like glade, with tall trees reaching their high canopies of leaves to the heavens. Fresh-smelling ferns waved in the wind. Mother sat down on the mossy log and untied the tea towel with the cookies inside. All talk ceased as everyone ate. Then Ralph spotted some wild grapes so they picked them and stuffed them into their mouths.

Belva finished her cookie and took a sip from the water jar. Sitting across from Grace, she suddenly frowned.

"Grace!" she exclaimed. "You've got a scratch. Or did a bug bite you?"

Glancing down, Grace saw a thin, red streak of blood trailing down the inside of her leg. Funny, she hadn't felt anything scrape her. She got up and went behind some bushes and hiked up her skirt to see exactly where the scratch started. Then she gasped. The source was higher up.

She knew what was happening to her. A year ago, Mother had taken her and Belva aside to explain what happened when a girl became a woman. Around age twelve or thirteen a girl's body matured. Biologically, she became a woman, capable of having a baby – not that it was something to do anytime soon. She would have a period every month, except when she was pregnant, until she was in her late forties or early fifties. Mother had showed the girls the pads she made for herself and kept in her lower bureau drawer.

Some girls called menstruation "the curse." Others called it "the blessing". Kathy called it "a visit from

Flo." Aunt Alice, a nurse, had given her the same information that Mother had provided to Grace and Belva, that getting your period was perfectly normal and just a detail to attend to, like combing your hair when you got up in the morning.

"But all that good information is of no help to me now," Grace thought. "If only Flo had timed her first visit better!"

She returned to the group and caught Mother's eye.

"I have to go home. I've forgotten something."

Mother looked puzzled for a moment; then she met Grace's gaze.

"Of course, my dear," her mother said. "Go ahead home. We won't be long. Here, take the dishtowel back with you."

Grace took the towel and strode back down the trail. Out of sight of the family she paused and went behind some bushes to check on "Flo". She didn't need the towel, not yet. Walking quickly, she emerged from the forest and saw, to her great relief, that nobody was outside Stonehurst. Aunt Alice and Uncle Fred's family must have gone to a beach. She took off her shoes, tiptoed up the outer stairs so as not to wake Father, then realized, with dismay, that to get a pad out of Mother's bureau drawer, she'd have to go into the bedroom and risk disturbing him.

She heard him call "Hello!" as she opened the door. There he was, up and dressed and leaning over the table, writing in India ink on a linen bedsheet.

"You're all out of breath," he remarked. "Is everything all right?"

"Fine. I just have to get something." She slipped into her parents' room and found the pads in the dresser drawer. When she emerged, her father was printing carefully in big letters. Grace looked over his shoulder.

"*In 1915*," she read, "*we buried 279 babies.*" Her jaw dropped. "Father, we didn't! What is this about?"

He put down his pen.

"This is my information sheet for my speaking tour," he told her. "I'll be talking about the need for better sanitary conditions in our cities. The government found money to fund the war, and now it should find money to make our communities safe from disease."

"What has that to do with dead babies?" she blurted.

"It's a statistic about one of the cities where I'll be speaking," he said. "Do you remember when we were living in Winnipeg and Ralph got the summer complaint and nearly died?"

Grace cast her mind back to her childhood. She remembered that Ralph, who had been the baby at that time, got sick and kept throwing up and crying. Mother, Auntie and the hired girl all took turns rocking him and giving him boiled water so he wouldn't dehydrate. The doctor gave up on him, but Mother wouldn't give up on him, and he got better. Every member of the family was thankful. But many babies and young children who got this flu-like illness didn't survive.

"The summer complaint is the result of heat, too much manure in the streets and too many flies spreading germs," her father said. "But that's what happens when you have crowded living conditions with no bathrooms and no running water. Epidemics don't have to happen. Local government can put in sewers and a water system, pay for better street cleaning, and even build decent housing. That's what this information sheet is all about."

Grace nodded. She'd just remembered something else from her early childhood in Winnipeg. She recalled standing in a green park, wearing her white organdie gown, holding her mother's hand. The park was a cemetery, she knew now, but at the time she'd been too young to understand what was going on, except that it was sad. A woman whom Grace's family knew, a member of the community, was crying so hard her body shook with sobs. Her husband, who was weeping too, had his arms around her. Father, in his best suit and clerical collar, stood at the graveside to say a final prayer for a little girl who had died.

"*The Lord giveth and the Lord taketh away,*" he began. Then his voice faltered and tears filled his eyes.

"No," he said. "No, I can't say that the Lord was responsible for this baby's death. To say so is blasphemous. It isn't God who made this baby die, it's Man, who won't take action to clean up the places in our city where disease originates and spreads."

Then he began the Lord's Prayer and the cluster of people joined in.

Grace's memory of this incident had been buried until now. Tears rose in her eyes. She felt a surge of admiration for her father, printing so carefully.

"Please write often while you're away," she said. "Mother always reads us parts of your letters."

"Of course I will." He looked up and smiled at her.

The others came thudding up the outside stairs. Grace quickly put the lid on the ink bottle before somebody knocked it off the table.

CHAPTER EIGHT

That afternoon, when Mother announced that she and Aunt Alice and the children were all going for a stroll, Grace offered to stay home to keep an eye on Howard when he woke from his nap.

"Thank you, dear. Maybe you'd like to take a nap, too."

Mother thought she wanted to stay home because she wasn't feeling well. Actually, she was fine, but wanted to listen in on a conversation. Uncle Fred and Father had just settled on the downstairs veranda to have one of their talks. Grace had picked out a quiet spot, in a wicker chair at the end of the veranda, shaded by a flowering shrub, where she would mend her skirt while listening and learning. Hearing her father and Fred talk was as informative as attending a public lecture.

Uncle Fred had settled into his rocking chair, with a glass of what looked like cold tea on the veranda ledge. He lit his pipe. Father, across from him in an armchair, had a cup of steaming coffee.

"I hear you're starting a new career," he began. "One that suits your talents."

"Yes. It's largely thanks to Will Ivens in Winnipeg."

Back in Winnipeg days, Grace had met the Reverend Mr. Ivens. Like Father, he had been a Methodist minister, but when he opposed the church being used to recruit soldiers during the war, the governing body fired him. Mr. Ivens then went out and started a "Labour Church". Working people and their families flocked to it to hear what Father called the "social gospel."

If someone asked Grace what that term meant, she would say it meant that people should take Jesus's message of love and brotherhood out into the world. Worshipping in church was fine, but not enough. How to do this? Giving money to charity helped, but you also had to support decent wages, improved sanitation, education and housing, and a social safety net.

The phrase "social safety net" had puzzled her until she asked Father to explain. She'd told him that it made her think of tightrope walkers and the song about the daring young man on the flying trapeze who flew through the air with the greatest of ease.

"Most people are tightrope walkers," Father had said. "One minute you can feel as if you're soaring through the air, completely carefree, and then your luck can change. You can lose your job or get sick, or get old and have no way to support yourself and your family. That's why the country needs a safety net, to catch people when they fall. Things like old age pensions, unemployment insurance, and decent wages that allow people to save would make up the safety net – if we had one."

Mr. Ivens and Father shared the same ideas, and Grace was pleased that he'd chosen Father to send on a lecture tour.

Now she tuned in to the conversation between Father and Dr. Fred.

"To put it in a nutshell," Father was saying, "I'll be talking about how to build a Canada where everyone gets a fair share and no one is left behind."

"I hope you'll talk about the war we've just come out of," said Uncle Fred. "Remind your audiences that its roots were in colonialism and imperialism. Rich industrialists pressured their governments to capture new colonies for them to exploit. The great powers of Europe carved up Africa in 1884. The scramble for colonies brought Germany nose to nose with Britain and France."

"I don't doubt your analysis, Fred, but I want to focus on Canada and its future." Father sipped some coffee.

"People have to understand the big picture," Uncle Fred insisted. "We keep hearing that the war was a great and glorious sacrifice in aid of freedom, but it was just poor fellows dying in the mud for an unworthy cause. And the Borden government is running the country as if the war were still on, though the Armistice was last November and a peace conference is going on in France."

"I'll definitely speak of how the federal government still rules by Orders-in-Council under the War Measures Act," Father said.

"The War Measures Act! Bah!" growled Fred. "Canada was never in any danger of invasion by Germany, yet under that Act the government imprisoned eight thousand newcomers to this country merely because they were born in countries that took the German side in the war. Now, James, on a related topic, you ought to remind your audiences of how Prime Minister Borden's government manipulated the electoral process with his Wartime Elections Act. He was so determined to bring in conscription that he gave the federal franchise to women, but not all women, only to the female relatives of men fighting overseas, because he knew they were likely to vote for him. And he took away the vote from a lot of men born outside Canada."

Father nodded. "We all know that a woman's right to vote wasn't uppermost in Mr. Borden's mind when he brought in that legislation, but that law led to a better one passed last year giving federal voting rights to all Canadian women over 21."

Grace, listening intently, resolved to vote when she was of legal age. She hoped there would be a working people's party to vote for by then.

"I'll mostly talk about the realities that everyday people face," Father went on. "Workers made some wage gains during the war, but in the six months since the Armistice, prices have shot up and consequently those wage increases count for nothing."

Fred nodded. "Inflation affects everyone. It's what has workers so angry in Winnipeg and other cities. Also, the flu epidemic last year was the last straw for many folks."

Grace remembered last winter's flu epidemic all too well. It had swept the world, including the Landing. People had died. She and all the other kids at Stonehurst got sick at the same time, so the grown-ups set up twelve cots in the big room downstairs and took turns nursing the children. Grace remembered vomiting and burning with fever, but she'd been lucky; they all had; no one in Kathy's family or hers died. Mother had been particularly worried about Ralph, who was the frail one, but he'd survived. None of the adults at their house got sick, though all of them went out into the community and tried to help those who were stricken.

"All through the war," continued Uncle Fred, "people tightened their belts, worked hard and mourned the loss of their loved ones. They read in the papers about war profiteering – the rich getting richer on the backs of working people. Then, when the end was in sight, along came the influenza. People are in a desperate mood. I think a revolution is just around the corner."

"Let's hope it's a bloodless one," Father said mildly.

"What do you think of this new League of Nations?" Fred asked.

Grace had heard of the League of Nations, an idea originating with the American president, Mr. Woodrow Wilson. He'd proposed it at the peace conference going on at Versailles, France.

Father's face lit up at the mention of it.

"It's a ray of hope."

He went on to say that the old-fashioned balance-of-power politics was dangerous. The only hope for humanity was for countries to join the League, banding together to keep peace. No more networks of alliances; no more squabbling over colonies.

"I especially like the idea that members of the League will never use force against each other," Father added. "They'll unite to help any member country that is attacked, and force the aggressive nation to back down."

Uncle Fred's furry eyebrows arched.

"I don't know if that will really happen, James. Right now, at the peace conference, France and England are blaming Germany for the war and they're going to punish her by breaking her economy. The League of Nations is a nice idea, but I still pin my hopes on the workers of the world uniting."

From above, Grace heard a cry. A passing gull? No, a child. It was Howard, waking up and feeling lonely. She dashed upstairs to look after him.

* * *

That evening was sad because Father was leaving tomorrow. He'd leave before they got up. She sat on the floor near his chair during family story time. Howard was already in bed for the night and Bruce dozed on Father's lap.

Mother opened *The Railway Children* at her bookmark. For years she had been reading aloud to the children before bedtime, and this latest storybook was one Grace had suggested. Grandma had mailed it to her for Christmas. She loved it and knew the younger children would, too. Mother read with such expression that the tale came alive.

First published in the year Belva was born, *The Railway Children* was about three children, Phyllis, Peter and Bobbie (a girl), who lived in big house in London, England. Their dad had an important government job in the Foreign Office. He was home most evenings, though, and the children loved their time with him. Then one evening some men came and took him away, leaving the children upset and confused. Their mum went to bed for two days, and when she finally pulled herself together she announced that they were going to have to leave London and to live in the country in a smaller house near a railway line.

"*We'll have to play at being poor for a while,*" she said, but their shortage of money was no game; it was very real.

Charles leaned forward.

"That's like us, now, ever since we left the manse," he said.

Mother paused.

"It's a little like us, yes, but we have plenty to eat and we're rich in all the things that matter."

"Like what?" asked Ralph.

"Well, your father and I are rich in children." Mother winked at Father. "And you children are fortunate to have a father who wants to make the world a better place."

"Is that why the railway children's dad went away, to make the world better?"

Charles asked this question of Grace, as he knew she'd read the novel.

"Actually, no," she replied. "We learn later that he was taken to prison, accused of spying for the Russians."

Charles's eyes widened.

Mother read the part about the family following the horse and cart that carried their belongings in the darkness across a field to their new home.

"That's like us," said Charles, "when we moved here."

Grace glanced at Father, wondering if he wanted to be reminded of that move. He was leaning back in his chair with his eyes closed. Now Mother was closing *The Railway Children*.

"Bedtime," she said.

Father's eyes flicked open and he shifted the sleeping Bruce in his arms. The children came up to him and kissed him goodnight, with Grace waiting until last.

"Write to us about your speaking tour," she whispered. "I wish you didn't have to go, though. I hate goodbyes."

He gave her at tired smile.

"A goodbye means that we have another hello to look forward to," he said. "We're never really apart because we are in each other's hearts."

CHAPTER NINE

At noon hour the following day, Grace sat alone under the arbutus tree in one corner of the school yard, admiring her gently-used new boots from the Winch family. She'd eaten her lunch alone because Kathy and Anna both had to go home at noon hour and Belva was talking to her friend Mary, who was twelve, like she was, and also in the Grade 8 Entrance class.

Mary's mother was Salish, her father English, and they fished for a living. They lived in a cabin on the outskirts of the village, but often visited a bigger settlement, a native village where Mary saw her maternal grandparents and extended family. They lived in a big cedar dwelling flanked with totem poles.

Often, at the dinner table at home, Belva told the family about Mary's people. There used to be a big celebration, the potlatch, in which many families gathered together to feast and give gifts. It sounded like Christmas to Belva. She'd been shocked to learn that the Canadian government had banned the potlatch years ago.

Mother was glad Belva was learning about Mary's traditions and said Belva was lucky to have Mary as a friend. Today, the younger girls weren't talking about native customs, though, but about Belva's future plans. She was saying she hoped to go to university to become a home economist. Grace listened, with curiosity. She didn't share her sister's fondness for domestic science; in fact, she didn't like cooking and sewing. She and Belva were sisters, yet so different!

Grace looked up at the arbutus, a marvellous tree. The leaves didn't turn colour and fall in the autumn, but stayed green all year, with new leaves coming as the old ones went away. Now the tree was in bloom with florets that looked like bunches of lily-of-the-valley. So beautiful!

"Hey, Belly-Button," she heard someone call.

This less than beautiful form of address came from Tommy Smith, strolling toward Belva and Mary. "Belly-button" was his name for Belva when teachers were not around.

As he joined the two girls in his class he looked Belva up and down.

"Hey," he said. "There's something odd about you today."

Belva turned pink. Grace wondered if she had a crush on Tommy? He had light brown curly hair and was always well-dressed, for his mother was a seamstress. She'd cut down Tommy's father's clothes and made them over for Tommy on her Singer treadle machine.

"You're wearing boys' clothes." He pointed at Belva and snickered. "That's a boy's sweater you have on, just like mine. See."

It was true. The V-necked brown pullover that Tom was wearing was very like the wine-coloured one that Belva had on, from the bag of clothes from the Winch family. Belva's colour deepened from pink to scarlet.

Tommy wasn't flirting, he was bullying. Grace rose and went over to the group.

"Here's another of the glad-rags gang," he announced. "This one is wearing boys' boots." He laughed gleefully. "Hey, everybody! Grace is wearing boys' boots."

As other children gathered around, Grace stared at him. What had gotten into him? He never used to be so mean, not when they were in the Methodist Sunday School together.

Then she remembered that when Father got into trouble for refusing to preach in favour of the war, Mrs. Smith had sided with those who had wanted him removed. Even though Father had resigned and was now in Vancouver, Tommy still had it in for Grace's family.

"Grace's wearing boys' boots," he repeated.

For a moment Grace wished Charles was strong enough to pick a fight with Tommy to defend the family honour, but Charles was only ten, and Tommy, thirteen. Anyway, Mother would be horrified to find her son rolling around in the dirt pummelling another boy. And while Father approved of vigorous debate, he didn't like physical fighting unless it was in a boxing ring where the two combatants abided by the Marquess of Queensbury rules.

"What's going on here?" demanded Anna, putting her hand on Grace's shoulder. Anna was taller and stronger than any of the other girls in Grace's class. She was the fastest runner and the strongest swimmer in their age range. She could beat the tar out of Tommy Smith if she tried, but then she'd get punished for fighting.

Grace took a deep breath. She stepped out where the other children could see her, stuck out first one foot, then the other, to show off her new boots.

"These boots are as good as new." She spoke in a carrying voice so all could hear. "They, and Belva's sweater, were gifts from friends in Vancouver. And, since I'm a girl, and I'm wearing these boots, then they're girls' boots. And since Belva is a girl, and she's wearing a sweater, then that makes her sweater a girl's sweater."

"That's right," chorused Anna and Kathy.

"In fact, almost everything I'm wearing was a gift from someone else," continued Grace to the crowd that had gathered around her. "My sweater used to belong to Kathy, here, but it was too small for her so she gave it to me. Thank you, Kathy."

Kathy looked pleased. "You're welcome."

"My dress used to belong to my Auntie in Winnipeg and this past winter Mother cut it down and made it smaller to fit me," she said. "The ribbon in my hair was a gift from Anna, here. Thank you, Anna."

Anna blushed. "You're welcome, I'm sure."

"My socks came in a shipment of used clothing from the Eastern provinces to the Methodist Church when Father was still serving there. Since no one else wanted them, and they fit me, I took them." Then, noticing Belva cringing with embarrassment, she said, "I'm going to stop there, except to say that hand-me-downs are good."

"You're a Second-hand Rose," he jeered.

"*Waste not, want not,*" Grace declared. "Being economical, saving when you can, is the smart thing to do. Belva doesn't like waste any more than I do. She's going to be a Home Economist."

His jaw dropped. "An e-communist? What's that?"

"The word is *Economist*!" Grace said sternly.

Kathy started to giggle and Grace couldn't help but join in the laughter as they walked toward the school door. Deep down, though, she was troubled, because it had just dawned on her why Tommy was so mean.

Part of it was anger over his father's death. Tommy's dad and uncle had enlisted back in 1914 at the start of the war. The family had come to Canada from England a few years earlier, and when war was declared, they felt a duty to go to England's aid, and were confident of an early victory.

Then, in 1916, word came that Mr. Smith had been killed at Vimy Ridge. In this big battle, Canadian soldiers had taken a height of land away from the Germans. The French and British troops had tried and failed to do this, but the Canadians succeeded, and made it possible for the Allies to advance. Losses had been heavy, though, and Mr. Smith had been shot and killed. Mrs. Smith and Tommy wanted to hear that Mr. Smith had died for a glorious cause, but Father didn't believe that the cause had been glorious. He thought the war was the result of the scramble for colonies and power, and a terrible waste of lives. In good conscience, he couldn't say what would have made the Smiths feel better.

The war had ended on November 11, 1918. When Tommy's uncle, his mother's brother, arrived home, Grace had been standing on the sidelines when the townsfolk gathered at the government wharf to welcome him off the steamship. He'd walked tall in his khaki uniform and although he looked thin and tired, he had no missing limbs or visible scars. He took his sister's arm, Tommy held his hand, and the three of them walked to the Smiths' house.

Through Grace had been past the house often, going to and from Anna's place, she'd never seen Tommy's uncle outdoors. She hoped that having him home made Tommy feel better. An uncle wasn't the same as a father but it was something. Meanwhile, she tried to avoid Tommy, which was easier said than done since they went to the same school and lived in a village.

After school that day, Grace spent an hour on homework in Mother's classroom, then headed up the hill to Anna's house so that the Kangas family could practise their English with her. She took the long way so as not to run into Tommy.

Grace had first met Anna at a meeting to do with the proposed co-op store. Soon after that, Mrs. Kangas started coming to the afternoon English classes that

Father and Mother used to hold at the manse, back when Father was still the Methodist minister. Anna's parents also attended the community get-togethers that Father organized in the hope of bringing together the people of Finnish background, who lived on the hillside, and the older residents, mostly of English background, who lived near the harbour. When Father left the church and went to work in Vancouver, these programs came to an end. Once Mother got hired to teach, she was too busy to continue the conversational English lessons.

Anna, who was eager to perfect her English and go on in school, asked Grace if she would come to her house and help her, her mother, and her two younger sisters, practise their English. Flattered to be asked, Grace had said "Yes."

The Kangas family lived on the cliff overlooking the harbour. Mr. Kangas worked at a sawmill and was home on weekends. Mrs. Kangas and the girls tended a large garden.

On an earlier visit, Anna and her mother together told Grace a fascinating story about where they had lived before coming to the Landing. When Anna was a baby, they had lived on Malcolm Island, farther north, as part of a community called "Sointula", which meant "place of harmony".

Now, up ahead, was Anna's house, peaked-roofed, wooden and painted red, with the door and window frames whitewashed. Before Grace could knock, the door swung open.   "Welcome!" cried Anna.

The fragrance of fresh bread with plum preserves welcomed her. At the table sat the two little girls, each with a slate and slate pencil of chalk, ready to write down any hard words. Mrs. Kangas was tall, with high cheek bones, very like Anna, though with grey in her blond hair. The little girls had milk with their cookies, but Mrs. Kangas was making coffee, and served some with a lot of milk in it to Anna and Grace. At home, Grace and the other children weren't allowed coffee or tea, but here, it would be impolite to refuse it.

"Shall we work on verbs today, or just talk?" she asked.

"Let's talk," said Anna. "Let's ask each other questions. We'll take turns."

"Fine."

"All right. Where were you born?" Anna asked.

"In Winnipeg, Manitoba."

"Where were your parents born?"

"Both in Ontario."

"Do you have a *Mummo* and *Vaari*?" inquired little Helvi.

"Not here," Grace said. "I have a Grandma in Winnipeg, but my Grandpa died in the fall of 1917."

To her embarrassment, her eyes filled with tears.

"I miss him," she admitted. "At Christmas when he carved the turkey he always used to give me the wishbone. After dinner he'd tell us stories about his travelling missionary days among the settlers and Indians."

She didn't mention that he had died just after Father published a letter in the *Winnipeg Free Press* explaining his objections to National Registration, the first step toward conscription – and the first step to Father losing his job in Winnipeg. Grandfather was used to his eldest son's active conscience, but he was old and ill, and the controversy must have made his last months difficult.

Mrs. Kangas passed Grace a plate of oatmeal cookies.

"What do you want to be when you grow up?" she asked.

"A French teacher," Grace replied promptly. "My mother studied French and I really like learning another language."

"Good for you," said Mrs. Kangas. "Now it's your turn to ask the questions."

"I like hearing about Sointula. Tell me more," Grace urged.

Anna laughed. "I don't remember it. When we left there I was only a baby."

"My father said it was a socialist community. Was it?" asked Grace.

Mrs. Kangas nodded. "When I first come – came – to Canada, it was to Nanaimo where my man worked in the coal mines. Then we moved to Malcolm Island to start a community. There we planned to farm and cut wood and share what we grew and made, like a big family. Our leader, Matti Kuirikka, came from Finland to lead Sointula. Very smart man."

"It sounds like the early Christian communities," remarked Grace.

Mrs. Kangas frowned and shook her head.

"No. *Not* Christian. *Socialist*."

Then she broke into Finnish, speaking rapidly and with confidence. Anna translated.

"Mami says that in Finland the church was run by the landlords and other rich people. They underpaid and cheated poor people, then preached to them to be obedient and to work hard without complaining. The poor people in Finland gave up on the church and turned to socialism. At Sointula the settlers wanted a good community of peace and brotherhood and sisterhood. Everything shared. No one poor and hungry."

Grace nodded.

Mrs. Kangas interrupted. "We Finns like your father and mother. They are good people. They helped us during the flu."

"They were glad to," Grace said.

During the epidemic, when Grace's parents were sure that their own children, and those of Uncle Fred and Aunt Alice, were on the mend, they'd visited families in the village, including the homes of the Finnish settlers, and did whatever they could to help out, from consoling them to bringing food, airing the bedding, emptying pails and doing whatever household chores were necessary.

"Father learned a lot from the Finnish settlers here. To me, Sointula sounds wonderful. Why did you leave?"

"Too hard to make a living there," said Mrs. Kangas. "Also, a big fire in 1903 burnt us out." She added something in Finnish.

"She says she wanted us children to go to a good school," said Anna.

Grace couldn't think of any more questions to ask, so she encouraged the little girls, Helvi and Tula, to interview each other. After more cookies, she glanced at the clock and saw that she should go home.

"I'll walk part way with you," Anna offered, knowing that Grace was nervous passing Tommy Smith's house. Sometimes he lurked outside with a sling shot. Several kids had felt the sting of a stone striking them in the back if they had roused his anger.

To Grace's dismay, there he was, in his back yard, and holding his slingshot. When he noticed them he shouted, "Pacifists! Bolsheviks!"

"Bolshevik" was the political party that had taken over the government in Russia in late 1917. Ever since they'd reorganized Russia and executed the czar and his family, "Bolshevik" had become a bad word, worse than a swear word. But why would anyone would call her or Anna "Bolshevik"? "Pacifist", yes, because "pacifist" meant being in favour of peace, and her family was on the record as being that. But Bolsheviks lived in another country on the other side of the globe.

Anna stopped in her tracks and stared fixedly at Tommy.

"Ignore him," murmured Grace. Anna ignored her.

"Come closer and say that," she shouted. "I dare you."

Smirking, Tom sauntered up to them.

"*Pacifist. Bolshevik.*"

Anna lunged at him. He swerved but she overpowered him, threw her arms around him in a grizzly bear hug, and wrestled him to the ground. Then she sat on him.

"Say you're sorry," she ordered.

"Sorry." The word was faint.

Anna reached into his pocket and took his sling shot.

"Now, go home and tell your mother she wants you," she said, getting off him.

Tommy slunk off home.

"Do you want the slingshot?" Anna asked Grace.

"No, you keep it."

* * *

That evening before bedtime, Mother read more of *The Railway Children*. In that night's episode, the mum in the story was sick, and the doctor recommended rest, medicine, and healthy food like fruit and milk. Though the children had no money, they had an idea. Every day when they watched the 9:15 train on its way to London, they saw an old gentleman looking out the window. They waved and he nodded. The children decided to ask him for help. They held up a sign reading: "Look out at the station" when he next went past in the train. Then they ran to the station, and, through the open window of the railway carriage, gave him a letter explaining the crisis and asking him to please bring them what they needed and leave it with the station master.

While listening, Grace observed her brothers' reactions. The little boys leaned forward, hanging on every word, and when the old gentleman did as he was asked, and more, by adding wine and roses, they clapped their hands in delight.

"Maybe the old gennelman can get their pa out of jail," Ralph suggested. "Is that what happens, Grace?"

"We'll have to wait and see," Grace said, as Mother closed the book.

"Can the next book be about buried treasure?" Charles wanted to know. "This one is all right, but I like adventure books about secret vaults and hideaways."

"We could read *Treasure Island*," Mother said.

In bed that night, Grace thought about the ending to *The Railway Children*. The old gentleman gets to know the children and is convinced that their dad is not a spy, so he sets about to prove their father's innocence. Having a father in prison was an awful disgrace for the family in the novel, even though he was falsely accused.

In real life, did good luck come along to save families? Grace wasn't sure. Father's posting to the church in the Landing had certainly been fortunate for the family. It was beautiful here, and you could practically live off the land and sea. Luck had smiled on them the other day, too, when the Winch family sent those good used clothes. But, in terms of Father finding a permanent career, they hadn't been so fortunate. Lecture tours eventually came to an end, and then how would Father earn money?

Mother was still up. Grace could hear the clink of a cup against a saucer. She was probably mending, a never-ending job because they couldn't afford new clothes. Mother was like the old woman who lived in a shoe who had so many children she didn't know what to do. Grace got up and tiptoed down the hall to the kitchen where she found her mother shortening the arms of the blue shirt for Charles.

"Can I help?" she asked, blinking in the light.

CHAPTER TEN

Mother looked up.

"Grace. Are you feeling all right?"

"Yes, but I can't sleep."

"Is this business of becoming a woman bothering you?"

Grace shrugged. "It isn't really bothering me. It's just that I don't feel ready to be a woman. I don't want to have babies, not for years yet, if ever."

"Well, of course you don't," Mother said promptly. "But isn't it nice to know that you can, someday, if you want to? I was always amazed at the way my infants developed. They were so fragile and helpless at birth, but soon showed their little personalities. For me it was a miracle, every time."

Grace sank onto a chair. "I guess."

"Someday you'll meet someone and fall in love and want to be with him all the time, and then you may feel differently about babies."

Grace took a button from the box, threaded a needle, and sewed it where it was needed on the front of Bruce's little shirt. Mother loved Father, but the part about being with him always wasn't working out so well. She was always the one left with the children while he was away.

"Mother, did you have any boyfriends before Father?" she asked.

Mother smiled.

"There was a neighbour boy I liked, when I was growing up on the farm at Cavan, but he was looking for a good farmer's wife, and I wanted to be a teacher. My father said that, instead of giving me a dowry when I got married, he would pay my way through school as far as I wanted to go, and I accepted his offer."

"So then you went to the University of Toronto?" Grace supplied.

"First I went to Normal School, then taught for a while, and then went to the University of Toronto from 1898 to 1901 to become a high school teacher. Those of us who graduated in '01, *naught one*, were nicknamed *The Naughty Ones*."

"Did you go out with boys at university?" Grace inquired.

"Yes." Mother stopped sewing and got a far-away look in her eyes. "I was one of only a few women students, so we girls were much in demand. But we weren't at all naughty. We had very high standards of behaviour. I remember one brash young man who took me skating, asking if he might call me *Lucy*. I said, *Certainly not!* because I thought he was being too forward."

Grace giggled. "How oldfashioned!"

"It does sound oldfashioned by today's standards."

"And then Father came along and you married him."

Mother had a faraway look.

"It wasn't quite like that. I boarded with a girl named Clare and when she told me that her cousin was coming from Manitoba to study at Victoria College and would be staying at the same boarding house as we were, I wasn't pleased. I thought he'd intrude on our studies and take up all of Clare's time. Clare assured me that James was a quiet, studious philosophy student and wouldn't be a nuisance at all."

"Was it love at first sight?" Grace asked.

Mother shook her head. "It was *liking* at first sight. Your father renewed old acquaintance with his cousin, Clare, and another cousin named Charlie, and we four went out as a group, I as Charlie's partner and James escorting Clare. On those double dates, I learned more about your father and was very impressed. He was already an ordained minister in the Methodist Church, and a university graduate, and he planned to go to England to study at Oxford, one of the greatest universities in the world."

Grace nodded. She had heard pieces of this story but never the whole tale at one time.

"James wasn't at all stuck-up," Mother continued, "even though he came from a highly respected family. His father was head of the Methodist Church in western Canada and had seen to it that his eldest son received a wealth of experience. James grew up on the prairies and led an outdoor life as you children do now. When he was old enough, his father took him on his travels for the church. They travelled by horseback and camped out much of the time, and your father got to see the west. Later, James served as a summertime minister in southwestern Manitoba and was touched by the hard lives of the settlers there. I learned so much from his stories and was moved by his dedication. Then, after a year, he went to England."

"To Oxford. Did you miss him?"

"Yes, but I didn't let on. He wrote the three of us letters about the war fever going on in Britain at the time. Men were being urged to join the British army to fight to protect mining companies' interests in South Africa, and James was appalled. He also told us about his field placement at a settlement house, a mission in the East End of London, and the programs it offered to people in the slums."

"It sounds like the Stella Avenue mission in Winnipeg," Grace said.

Mother beamed.

"Right you are! Your father remembered what he learned there and later, in Canada, he was a natural choice to head a similar community centre. The slums in England horrified him. He didn't see why a big new country like Canada should have any slums at all."

"Did you write to him when he was in England?"

"Occasionally."

"Love letters?"

"No. Friendly letters. I told him of my graduation in 1901 and of my first teaching position in a high school. Then Charlie asked me to marry him. I was completely surprised. I had to say no, that I wasn't in love with him, and I blurted out that I loved James."

Grace's mouth fell open. She had never heard this part of the story before.

"James came back to Canada and served in two pastoral charges out west. He was always on my mind, and we wrote to each other, but it seemed as if life had separated us forever. Meanwhile, in 1902, when he was an assistant minister in Winnipeg, he wrote to Charlie that he wanted to get out of the ministry and run a settlement house. Charlie wrote back and said he need a loving wife and should come east to find one. Then he told James that I loved him."

"So then Father came to Ontario and you got married," prompted Grace.

Mother shook her head.

"Not so fast. Your father wrote to me, and I replied, and our letters became deeper and more personal. He came east in September 1903 when I was teaching at Lindsay Collegiate. I packed a lunch in a wicker basket, met his train, and took him out in the country for a picnic. We picked up our conversation where we'd left off and it was as if he'd never been away. By the end of the day we were engaged to be married."

"So then came your wedding at our grandparents' farm in Ontario."

Mother laughed. "Again there was a delay of a year. You see, I'd signed a contract to teach, and we both needed to save some money. A year later we were married at my parents' farm in Cavan, with Charlie as the best man and Clare, the bridesmaid. We honeymooned in Muskoka, then caught the train to Winnipeg."

"And then you had me." Grace smiled.

"Yes, the following year we had you. I was thirty, and some people thought I was going to be an old maid. I felt so happy to be married to the man I loved, and being a mother was the icing on the cake."

"Are you still glad you married him?"

"I certainly am," Mother said, with a smile. "Now, my dear, you should go to bed. Before you go, I must mention that I have an evening meeting coming up some time next week, and I'll need you and Belva to sit with the younger children. They'll be in bed, and Fred and Alice will be downstairs in case of emergency."

"That's fine. Belva and I will do our homework. Where are you going?"

"It's a school meeting."

Frown lines appeared in Mother's forehead as she spoke.

"Now, Grace, do go back to bed. You look tired."

Settling into bed, remembering the shadow that had come over her mother's face, Grace wondered what the meeting was about.

CHAPTER ELEVEN

"**I** have a surprise," Kathy announced, as she met Grace outside the house the next morning. "Mama wants to go to Vancouver tomorrow and stay overnight with friends. She says we can go with her."

"Wonderful!" Grace exclaimed. Then her grin faded. She was needed at home. There were chores to be done. Besides, she'd have to miss two days of school. And she didn't have any spending money.

"Ask your mother," Kathy urged.

The girls ran to school, found Mother writing on the board, and asked permission. Mother thought for a minute.

"Why not?" she said. "I'm sure it will be educational."

The following day, dressed in her newest middy blouse, blue pleated skirt and best black stockings, and carrying a satchel containing a clean nightgown and underwear, Grace, with Aunt Alice and Kathy, boarded the Union Steamship vessel *Chilco* at the government dock. The *Chilco* and its sister ship, the *Chasina*, made runs between Vancouver and Port Neville, stopping at several harbours in between, including the Landing. As the steamship made its way out of the harbour, Grace stood on deck, looking in all directions.

Gazing at snow-capped Mount Elphinstone, she thought of the young men who had camped somewhere on its slopes during the war. After the conscription bill passed in 1917, some men of army age decided they weren't going to be forced to go to war, and stole away into the bush on the mountain slope. Their exact location was hush-hush. The only reason Grace knew about it was that Anna's father was among the locals who took them food. According to Anna, the conscription dodgers built themselves log cabins and stayed out of sight, and the Royal Northwest Mounted Police never came after them. Now that the war was over, Grace guessed they'd quietly left the mountain to look for work.

Kathy, on deck beside Grace, drew her attention to a paddle-wheeler pulling a log boom, a vast bunch of floating logs kept together by a circle of big logs, chained together, all of them being pulled down the strait to the mills of Burrard Inlet, where they would become lumber. The logs were five feet thick, as thick as Grace was tall, and up to 200 feet long. Grace felt a rush of admiration for the captains of these tow boats.

In storms, she'd heard, the crews would cut the tow lines and make for the nearest harbour, leaving the log boom to bounce up and down in the waves. A boat could easily be dashed to pieces against the logs it was pulling. When the storm was over the boat would go back out to see what was left of the boom, and to attach it again and continue on the journey. Often, however, the force of the water broke up the booms and eventually the logs floated toward shore with the tides. Then, salvagers, also known as "beachcombers", would go out in their boats, usually little steamboats or even wooden dories, and would collect the stray logs to sell to a mill. It was finders-keepers.

Aunt Alice, shading her eyes, said she longed to see a pod of whales. Orcas, the black and white killer whales, were no strangers to the Sunshine Coast, but Grace had seen only one from a distance. She'd spotted it one Sunday when she and Charles and Father were travelling in the *Goodwill* to a church service at Sechelt.

Aunt Alice went into the cabin to sit down, but the girls didn't want to miss any of the sights. Pulling their tam-o-shanters over their ears, and tying their scarves firmly, they took in everything. They saw fishing boats carrying salted herring across the Pacific to faraway Japan. Nearing Vancouver were splendid yachts owned by rich people, and Canadian Pacific ocean liners carrying silk and tea from China. It made Grace proud that her father's labour helped these goods get distributed across North America. Closer to the Vancouver harbour they saw Salish people paddling along the shoreline near the city.

Grace spied a motor launch that reminded her of the *Goodwill*, the twenty-five foot gas-powered boat owned by the Methodist Church. When her father was still a Methodist minister, he used it to travel from the Landing to other communities on the coast and on Howe Sound. She'd loved it when Father invited the whole family to come along with him on a Sunday.

How refreshing, to be out on the water, to lean back, close her eyes and feel the wind and salt spray in her hair!

She remembered one trip, when her reverie was interrupted by a "Hey!" from Charles. Opening her eyes, she looked where her brother was pointing.

"Porpoises!" he'd cried, and sure enough, these black and grey sea creatures with white underbellies were frolicking in the waves. All the children craned their heads to look except for Howard, asleep on Mother's lap.

Then they'd heard a chug and a snort – not the sound of any sea creature they knew, but the *Goodwill*'s motor conking out. Either the *Goodwill* hadn't been in the best repair, or Father hadn't been skilled in operating it. This wasn't the first time it had quit.

As Father started fiddling with the motor, Charles got a mischievous look on his face. Softly he began singing, "*Row, row, row your boat, gently down the stream.*" Mother glared at him, but of course the younger boys, Ralph and Bruce joined in.

"Stop that!" Father barked in his strongest pulpit voice.

"Hush, children." Mother's quiet tone meant business. The song faded.

Grace and Belva shaded their eyes and looked around, ready to wave if another boat came into sight. Father tried the motor again. It sputtered but did not catch.

"We're going to be late. The congregation will go home," Belva whispered. She began nibbling her fingernails.

"The motor is just flooded, that's all," Grace said softly. "We'll wait a while and try it again and it will go. Let's see who can think of the most hymns involving boats and the sea."

"*Will Your Anchor Hold Through the Storms of Life?*" Belva said.

"*Jesus, Saviour, pilot me, over life's tempestuous sea,*" Charles added.

"*Throw Out the Lifeline,*" said Ralph.

Grace glanced at Mother. Her eyes twinkled and her mouth twitched. Against her, young Howard breathed softly in sleep.

"Look. Look there!" Ralph pointed. Sure enough, a motor boat skimmed into view.

"You children stay put!" their father ordered. Carefully he stood up, took off his hat and waved it.

"It's coming," Grace breathed. "Help is on the way."

The motor boat grew ever larger until it was alongside the *Goodwill*. A Salish fisherman waved at them.

"Trouble?" he asked.

"It's the motor," Father said. "Can you help us?"

"Sure. I'll tow you to shore."

Remembering those days, Grace wished, for just a moment, that the family still had the use of the

Goodwill for adventures on the water, but then the sight of Vancouver, bordered by lush rain forest, captured her attention.

Soon they disembarked and were on a street car, heading for Woodward's Department Store. There were plenty of horse-drawn vehicles but also quite a few motor cars, something new. She saw a blue 1919 Buick touring car that she especially liked.

Vancouver had a Carnegie public library. What a great thing to be able to borrow books and read to your heart's content! Grace had already read everything in the book case at school. Vancouver also had three theatres, and she longed to see a play there. Ever since seeing a dramatic production by the Finnish theatrical group in the Socialist Hall at home, she had loved plays.

Once out of the street car and onto the wooden sidewalk, Grace and Kathy stayed close to each other and to Aunt Alice, because there were so many people bustling along, jostling each other. Grace saw Sikh men wearing turbans. She noticed an elegant lady wearing a Japanese kimono, her glossy black hair done up on her head in a bun fastened by two brightly painted sticks. Men in cloth caps and work clothes made her think of Father and wish she could see him.

Woodward's was a three storey building with an astonishing variety of goods. In its pharmacy department Aunt Alice found supplies that Dr. Fred needed. The section Grace liked best was women's and girls' clothing. Though she was happy to wear used clothing, and took Mother's word that "a pretty young girl looks good in anything", she had some mild interest in clothing styles. The newest dresses for young women did not have waistlines but were straight up and down, loose, with no need for corsets. Grace, who had never worn corsets and had never looked forward to doing so, was pleased with this fashion development. Hemlines were shorter, too. Grace, in her sailor blouse, was glad to see that the sailor style collar was still fashionable.

When Aunt Alice joined the girls she looked with interest at some of the new ladies' fashions, but didn't buy anything. She looked smart in her good outfit, a two-piece grey wool suit, with a calf length skirt and a straight-up-and-down jacket.

After their shopping, they went for lunch at a Chinese restaurant, where Grace had won-ton soup, chicken chow mein and chop suey. Then, after some window shopping, they caught another streetcar to the home of Mrs. Johnson, a former schoolmate of Aunt Alice's, now married to a university professor. She was waiting to greet them on the front porch of their two storey house surrounded by rose bushes.

"You're just in time for tea," she announced.

Grace's eyes drank in the furniture, made of reddish brown gleaming wood. She also liked the English bone china tea set with roses all over it. There were no fingerprints on the doorframes or scuff marks on the table legs, probably because the Johnsons had no children. From the kitchen came the delectable aroma of roast beef. She would have to save room for the evening meal and not have too many macaroons now.

Mr. Johnson, a scholarly-looking man with a Teddy Roosevelt pince nez, came into the parlour, accepted a cup of tea, and asked the girls about school. Both hoped to go to the University of British Columbia, where he taught.

"Maybe when you're ready to attend, we'll have a proper university campus," he said. "Now that the war is over, maybe some progress will be made."

Land had been cleared on Point Grey and the frame of the Science building had been built in 1914, but the coming of war brought construction to a halt.

"These days I teach in temporary buildings near the Vancouver General Hospital," he added. "When all the young college men return from their wartime service, these buildings will be crowded. This fall we may have to hold classes in the Sunday school rooms of churches, or even in tents."

"That would be fun," Grace exclaimed. "I'm going to study hard, and find out if ministers' children get reduced tuition."

"Oh," said Mrs. Johnson, "then you're one of the family living in the upstairs of Alice's home."

"So it's *your* father, my dear," said Professor Johnson, "who left the Methodist Church and is working as a stevedore."

Grace nodded.

"A man of his education and background!" exclaimed Mrs. Johnson.

Grace squirmed.

"Soon Father is going on a lecture tour of the western provinces," she said, wondering if a lecturer for the labour movement was more acceptable than a dock worker.

"Glad to hear it," said Professor Johnson. "I've heard your father speak and I admire what he is doing. Are you seeing him while you're in town?"

Grace shook her head.

"I didn't tell him I was coming. There wasn't time to send a letter."

"Could we reach him by telephone?" asked Professor Johnson. "I'd like to meet him and shake his hand. Where is he staying?"

"With the Winch family. Mr. Winch is head of the Labour Council."

The Professor turned to his wife. "Mr. Winch's office would have a telephone. Dear, let's invite Grace's father over here this evening."

"Certainly, if you'd like," said Mrs. Johnson.

"The telephone is in the kitchen, Grace. Come along and we'll get the operator to connect us."

The phone was attached to the wall, with a speaker that you talked into, and a receiver, on a hook at the side, that you put up to your ear. There was a little handle that you turned. Every telephone number was a combination of long rings and short ones, and no two numbers were alike.

The professor rang a long ring for the Operator and asked her to connect him to the Labour Council office. While she was doing so, he pulled out a stepping stool for Grace to stand on and put the receiver into her hand.

"Ernest Winch speaking," said a deep voice in her ear.

Grace introduced herself and thanked him for the bundle of clothing.

"You're welcome, little lady. Hold on, your Pa's here."

Grace's heart leapt. Then: "Grace?" Father's voice sounded worried. "Where are you? What's wrong?"

Hurriedly she explained. "Can you come and see me at the Johnsons? They'd love to meet you."

"I'm sorry, but I can't. I've been asked to address a meeting tonight."

Grace's heart sank. Then she heard him say, "On second thought, would you like to come and hear me and the other speakers?"

"Oh, yes, please!"

"Good. Bring Kathy, if she'd like to come. I'll meet you around six and say hello to the Johnsons. Give me the address."

When Grace returned to the parlour and explained, Mrs. Johnson rose and said she would hurry supper along so the girls could eat before Father arrived. But Kathy shook her head. She was pale, leaning against her mother's shoulder.

"I'm not feeling well and I'm not hungry," she murmured. "Auntie, may I go up and lie down?"

"Of course."

Alice felt Kathy's forehead. "She's not feverish. I expect she's just tired after a busy day."

Dinner was served at 5 p.m. and Aunt Alice came down to it, but reported that Kathy was asleep. Grace was too excited to eat. She was not only seeing Father, she was going to a meeting with him!

CHAPTER TWELVE

Grace kept a grip on Father's hand as they made their way through the crowd outside the hall. Inside, the place was even more packed, mostly with men, all much taller than she was. She smelled sweat, tobacco, shaving lotion and a whiff of alcohol.

"Hey, there, James!"

Men greeted Father warmly as if they knew him. One said, "Good evening, Miss," and suddenly shy, she murmured "Good evening" in return. She and Father made their way to the row of chairs nearest the platform where he would be speaking. A middle aged woman and a boy about Grace's age waved to him, and Father led her over to meet them. They were Mrs. Winch and her son Harold, the people who had given Grace's family the gently used clothing. Father introduced her and she said hello.

"Thank you for the boots," she told Harold. "They fit perfectly. Look." Grace pointed to her feet.

The boy turned red and muttered, "You're welcome."

"Come and sit by me, dear," said Mrs. Winch. "That's my husband up on the stage. He's head of the Vancouver Trades and Labour Council."

The meeting was called to order. Grace admired the way the speakers could project their voices in the large building. First, the chairman, Mr. Winch, announced that the speakers, as a panel, would take questions after all three had spoken. This gathering was like Father's public education nights at the Landing, only on a larger scale. The subject matter was similar – it was all about building a new society after the war was over, and about the opposition they would face in doing so.

The first speaker talked about the wealth of Canada. During the war, he said, the over-all wealth of the country, the Gross National Product, had doubled because of the demand for armaments and supplies for the armies overseas. It seemed wrong to him that an increase in wealth should result from cities being turned to rubble and people killed. Worse, this increase in the country's wealth wasn't being shared fairly among Canadians. The workers on farms and in factories who had produced the food products, machines, shells and ammunition were not rich as a result. Factory owners and war profiteers were.

"The Borden government asked everyday Canadians to send their men to war, but it didn't ask the rich to pay their fair share of this war," he declared. "Ordinary people sacrificed their lives; the rich should have sacrificed their wealth."

The next man spoke of current events. Canada's federal government seemed to be trying to turn the clock back, although the world was changing. The government had sent an army to join other western powers to fight against the new workers' government in Russia. Some Vancouver dock workers had refused to load supplies for these forces, bound for the north of Russia, and these workers deserved a round of applause.

The man at the podium looked at Father, who had refused to help load those ships, and as the audience clapped and whistled, Grace felt proud. The speaker went on to talk about countries where there was unrest that might lead to a change of government. When he spoke about Germany, Grace was startled to hear that one of the leaders who had agitated for change was a woman, Rosa Luxembourg. Continuing to listen, she learned to her dismay that this woman had been murdered along with another working class leader.

Turning to the political situation in Great Britain, the speaker mentioned the newly formed British Labour Party which hoped to form the next government.

"The winds of change are blowing, all over the world," he concluded. "Everyday people like ourselves are part of a wider movement to bring about a fair and just society." The room rang with applause.

Next it was Father's turn. He ran up the three steps onto the stage and shook hands with the previous speakers. Addressing the crowd as "brothers and sisters" he said he had moved to British Columbia from Winnipeg, Manitoba, two years earlier, and wanted to tell what he knew about the current labour situation in his old home town.

A year ago, in May 1918, the Winnipeg Trades Union Congress had been on the verge of calling for a general strike, and indeed some city employees – the firemen and teamsters – had gone out for a day or so, with railway workers joining them in sympathy. The war was still going on then and these workers were in a good bargaining position. Premier Norris of Manitoba and federal Labour Minister Gideon Robertson hadn't wanted a disruption of the war effort, so they'd met with labour, then told the Winnipeg City Council to agree to a settlement. The workers got much of what they asked for.

"That brief strike occurred last May when the war was still going on," Father repeated. "The war is over now, and wages are not keeping up with the cost of living. Soldiers are coming back looking for work. Working people in Winnipeg are in a no-nonsense mood, and there may be a big collision between employees and employers."

Father reviewed some important meetings and events in Winnipeg over the last few months. In December 1918, the Winnipeg Trades and Labour Council and the Socialist Party held a big meeting to discuss why Prime Minister Borden's government was still running the country by order-in-council, as if it were still at war. It was still censoring newspapers, imprisoning people whose mother countries had been on the German side in the war, and, in general, ruling like a dictatorship at a time when the world was moving towards more freedom and democracy.

Grace felt a ripple of excitement, or anger, emanating from the audience. Several shouted, "Hear, hear!"

"That meeting made the rich people in Winnipeg nervous," Father continued. "That's why the authorities did little or nothing to stop the attack on workers there this past winter."

He read a short excerpt from the labour paper in Winnipeg which described uniformed men on horseback running down a group of new Canadian workers on Market Street and chasing them down side streets and alleys. They ransacked the Socialist Party offices, set fire to books and papers and threw a piano out of a window. They broke into the home of a well-known socialist, Sam Blumenberg, where they bullied his wife and made her kiss the flag, the Union Jack. Then they broke into a meat-packing plant and wrecked it because it employed so-called "aliens," people not of British origin.

"This mob violence was egged on by the business elite," Father said. "If a strike comes, I'm confident that returned soldiers will support their class interest. Those from rich families will support the businessmen and factory owners, but soldiers who were working men before they went to war will be on the side of labour. But this incident shows what workers are going to be up against if they go on strike, so it's important that they be well-organized and self-disciplined."

He paused while the audience applauded.

"Good speaker," remarked someone near Grace. Grace smiled and pounded her palms together harder.

"Now, brothers and sisters," said Father, in his carrying voice, "you may not agree with what I'm about to say next."

A hush fell on the room. Father said that many in his audience had attended a recent labour conference in Calgary. He hadn't been present, but he had heard a lot about it, and knew that the "Wobblies" – the International Workers of the World – had been very persuasive about the need for industrial unions rather than craft unions. The I.W.W. favoured the general strike as the best form of labour action.

An industrial union, Grace knew, was one which included all the workers in a factory or other workplace, from those with no special skills to those who were highly skilled at a particular trade. If everyone in a factory or other workplace was part of one big union and a majority voted to go on strike, they could close the place tighter than a drum and make the owners listen to their needs.

"I understand the benefit of having industrial unions, and I recognize that a general strike can be a powerful weapon," Father declared. "But let's think in practical terms."

If all the workers in a city held a general strike; that is, if they all walked off the job at once, normal life in that city would grind to a halt, and the strike leaders could possibly force government and business to agree to better wages, working conditions and positive changes in society as a whole. But if a general strike failed, it could usher in a period of terrible punishment, with even more censorship, imprisonment and deportations than at present.

"Workers should think long and hard before they take such action," Father declared. "I believe that we must change society on many different fronts at once. The threat of a strike is one way. Another is to organize a party like the British Labour Party and elect candidates who care about working people, so that they will enact laws that make a fairer, better country. That would be the more gradual, safer choice, but it will take awhile." Then he paused. "But, when all is said and done, if the workers in Winnipeg go on strike, I'm on their side. I'm waiting, like everyone here tonight, to see what will happen there."

Then he bowed.

No one booed. The applause was thunderous. Grace waved at Father and he gave her a big smile and waved back. She couldn't wait to tell Mother how well his words had gone over.

CHAPTER THIRTEEN

"I wish Father were here." Belva spoke softly, so as not to wake the younger ones. "He'd go with Mother to the meeting and speak up for her."

Grace watched her twelve year old sister nibble her nails. Their homework was spread on the table between them, but neither could concentrate. Living in the village of Gibson's Landing, she'd always felt that the mountains shielded them from the turmoil of the outside world, but now she knew how childish that notion was. Tonight's school meeting was the latest in a series of troubles; apparently it had been looming for some time.

Grace first heard of the meeting when her friend, Anna, beckoned her aside after school.

"I'm sorry your mother's being called on the carpet," she'd whispered. "She's a wonderful teacher."

Grace's jaw dropped. "What?"

"Some people want her fired."

Then Anna spilled everything she'd heard. Grace thanked her for the information and said she couldn't walk home with her because she had to find Belva. She found her sister with her chums under the arbutus tree. Together they went to see Mother, who was in the school preparing lessons.

Grace repeated what Anna had said. "Is it true?"

Mother sighed. "I've done nothing wrong, so don't worry, and don't bother your little brothers about it."

"Did you mention this meeting in your last letter to Father?"

"He has enough on his mind," Mother said. "I can handle it."

Now, under Belva's gaze, Grace cleared her throat.

"Actually," she began, "it's just as well that Father isn't here. It's on account of him that they want to fire her."

Belva gasped. "Surely not!"

"Think about it. Father had to resign as pastor here because he was against the Great War. Some church people are still mad because he wouldn't urge men to enlist. They know Mother and Father were of one mind on that."

"Everyone in my class likes Mother." Belva's lips were trembling. "She's kind and explains things well."

Mother taught Belva's Entrance class in the morning, then in the afternoons went to the high school room for French, History and Art. Grace was proud of how she looked with her apron off, wearing her navy skirt and fresh white blouse, with her glossy dark hair done up high on her head. She embodied calmness and clarity. Grace was making great progress learning French grammar from her.

"Mother is a good teacher," she told Belva, "but some people don't care about that. They want to run everything in the village, and they disapprove of everything Father believes in. So if he were with her tonight, it wouldn't help her."

"I wish she wasn't all alone." Tears rolled down Belva's cheeks.

"She'll be fine." Grace spoke with more conviction that she felt. "When we misbehave she talks to us in a low, firm voice and makes us ashamed of what we've done. She'll use that tone on her critics."

They both grinned. But, shielded by her math book, Grace frowned, remembering one of her mother's sayings: *"Convince a man against his will; he's of the same opinion still."*

She'd seen that saying demonstrated at one of the community meetings Father had organized to bring the Finnish and English settlers together. This particular meeting, on the subject "Canada after the War", had led to a heated argument between a pale little man of English background who thought no sacrifice was too big for King and Country, and a brawny, red-haired man of Finnish origin who said Canada should never have been a part of the imperialist war. Beneath the carbide lamp that hung over the teacher's desk, the two men had been nose-to-nose. The audience in the shadowy classroom gasped, wondering who would strike the first blow. Father got the discussion under control, and neither man lashed out with his fists, but neither changed the other's opinion either.

Remembering that dark classroom, Grace had an idea. At night the room was always dim except for the pool of light around the desk. Could someone quietly slip into the meeting, unnoticed? Why not? Being there would be easier than sitting here worrying.

"Maybe my love and support will vibrate through the air to Mother and buoy her up," she thought.

Belva shook her head at the idea.

"Mother wants us here with the younger children. Besides, we're not allowed to go running around at night."

"Well, I want to know what's happening. I'll ask Kathy to come with me."

"Aren't you scared?"

"Of course not," Grace lied.

"All right, go, but Mother will be mad."

"She'll never know."

Grace's hands trembled as she buttoned her coat. She took a match from the match box, gathered her boots in her hand, and in the other, held her "bug", or homemade lantern, a lard pail with many holes that she had punched in the metal using a nail and hammer. Anna had showed her how. The candle inside was stuck to the bottom of the pail with wax.

She tiptoed downstairs to the ground floor and knocked on the door of Uncle Fred and Aunt Alice's sitting room. Kathy answered. She was still in her day clothes, not her nightgown. Good!

"Can you come out for a walk?"

"I'll ask." Kathy withdrew. A few minutes later she emerged, her eyes sparkling with anticipation, her "bug" in her hand.

"Are we going to the school?" she whispered.

"Yes."

"Good. Your mum shouldn't be facing her opponents alone. If my pa were here I'd ask him to come to support her, but he's out on a sick call."

"We won't make ourselves known. We'll just creep in and listen."

"Oh, eavesdropping! Goody! We're like Mata Hari."

Outside, they lit their candles. The moon made a silvery path on Howe Sound. Trudging up the hill, Grace's heart thudded with trepidation. Nearing the school, they saw a faint light in one classroom window. On the doorstep they tried the main door. Unlocked. So far, so good. They blew out their candles, slipped off their boots, stepped silently over the threshold and tiptoed toward the hum of voices from one of the classrooms. The door was open, and was at the rear, with the teacher's desk at the front, enabling them to slip in, unnoticed. As Grace had expected, the room was pitch dark except for the area near the desk.

Three men sat on chairs, their backs to the door. Grace recognized the bald one at the desk as the inspector from Vancouver, who must have made a special trip by ferry to be here for this meeting. Mother sat in a chair beside the desk. If she'd glanced toward the door she might have glimpsed two pale faces in the shadows, but she was paying attention to the inspector's words.

"Calling for the dismissal of a teacher is a serious matter," he was saying. "British Columbia has a teacher shortage at present, and not too many teachers want to come to an isolated hamlet like Gibson's Landing. You're fortunate to have Mrs. Woodsworth here in your midst. She has a Bachelor of Arts degree, a teaching certificate, and a wealth of experience."

"We *do* call for her dismissal." The speaker sounded stern. "She's a bad influence on the children."

"In what way?" asked the inspector.

"Her husband is a Bolshevik radical away on a speaking tour for the labour movement," the man declared. "He came here in 1917 as Methodist minister but he wouldn't support the Great War for God and Country because he's a pacifist. That comes close to treason."

The inspector's brow furrowed.

"That's *your* opinion," he said. "Bear in mind that the war is over now and a conference is going on in Paris to achieve a just peace settlement. The American president has issued fourteen points on which peace will be based. Most of us are eager to put the war behind us."

The head of the three-man delegation waved his hand.

"But think of what's going on in Russia. Mr. Woodsworth is friendly with the Finns, and everyone knows they're Bolsheviks."

The inspector cleared his throat.

"That's a sweeping statement," he said. "Can we really say that everyone from Finland is a Bolshevik? And please remember that James S. Woodsworth is not teaching in this school. This meeting isn't about him."

"He refused to pray for the Allied cause," said a man whom Grace remembered from churchgoing days.

Her fists clenched. What a lie! Father had prayed for the men overseas. He'd prayed for the war to end. He had asked God to take pity on all the people who were suffering and dying, soldiers and civilians. But, as Uncle Fred said, in wartime anyone who didn't beat the drum and wave the flag was in danger of being labelled "traitor."

"Again, what Mr. Woodsworth may or may not have said has nothing to do with Mrs. Woodsworth's work as a teacher," the inspector said firmly.

"He has indoctrinated his own children," the third fellow blurted. "One of them says that when she grows up she's going to be a communist."

Mother turned to him. "Really?" She sounded interested. "Which one?"

"Your younger girl."

Mother burst out laughing. "Belva wants to be a home *economist. Economist.* Not Communist."

"Even so, our children shouldn't be subjected to revolutionary ideas," the man said stolidly.

"That's right," said the head of the group.

Mother cleared her throat and looked him in the eye.

"I teach the curriculum set out by the Ministry of Education," she told him. "What revolutionary ideas am I supposed to have taught my students?"

Silence. Two of the men turned to the third, but no one spoke.

"Tell the inspector how many children, among you, you have in the school," Mother continued.

"My youngsters are grown-up," said the leader.

"My wife and I haven't been blessed with children," said another.

"My little lad started last fall," said the third.

The inspector nodded. "So, among the three of you, you have one child at the village school." He turned to Mother. "What grades do you teach, ma'am?"

"The Entrance class and the high school students."

"Gentlemen," said the inspector, "you have failed to convince me that Mrs. Woodsworth has done anything wrong. I've sat in on her classes and talked to some parents and everyone agrees she's doing a fine job. If you can't come with anything of substance to complain about, then you owe her an apology."

Grace exhaled. Mother wouldn't lose her job. They'd have money coming in regularly. She nudged Kathy. They stole out, found their boots on the front step, and started home. Halfway down the hill, they paused and looked back. In the moonlight they saw two figures outside the school, one with a white blouse that gleamed in the dark. She guessed the inspector was having a final word with Mother.

"Thank you, Kathy, for coming with me," Grace said softly. "I feel better now."

"I'm so glad your mum is keeping her job," Kathy murmured.

Back in their apartment on the second storey of Dr. Fred's house, Grace found Belva pacing the floor in agitation.

"All's well," she whispered. "Mother is still in work."

Belva's frightened look vanished. "What a relief!"

A few minutes later, when Mother came in, the girls were bent over their books.

"How did it go?" Grace asked innocently.

Mother made a face.

"Oh, it was just so jolly! The delegation ended up apologizing to me. I'll go to school tomorrow with a lighter heart."

The girls sprang up and hugged her.

That night, as Belva slept, Grace lay awake, brooding. The Great War had killed so many people, turned neighbour against neighbour, brought the flu epidemic and had driven up the price of everything. Father was trying to make the world a better place, but had he gone too far out on a limb?

CHAPTER FOURTEEN

The following day, it was Belva's turn to go right home to take care of Howard after the housekeeper left, and Kathy joined her to keep her company. Grace went into her mother's classroom, where they usually worked in companionable silence, her mother preparing lessons and Grace doing homework. That day, however, Mother had her books and papers packed in her satchel.

"Hello, dear," she said. "I need your help."

"Oh? With what?"

Mother took a folded paper from her pocket. "This is a note from Mrs. Smith, asking me to send home Tommy's homework. He has missed two days now and she doesn't want him to fall behind and fail his English Entrance exam."

"Oh, no!" Grace shook her head. "I'm not going to take his homework to him. He and his mother don't like us, and, besides, he has a sling shot – or he did, till Anna took it from him. He has probably made another by now."

"*I'm* taking his work to him," Mother said. "As his teacher, it's my duty to explain what he missed. His class is learning how to analyze sentences, and parsing can be difficult. All I want from you is your company. The visit will go more smoothly if you're along."

Grace made a face. "I can't see how it will. Tommy doesn't like me and his mother supported that group in the church that wanted Father to resign."

"All the more reason for me to do the right thing. Mrs. Smith is more likely to be polite if I have one of my children with me, and that's why I need you along."

"What about Charles? He gets along with everyone."

"But you're my oldest, my right hand girl, and I'd like you with me."

Grace sighed. "All right. I'll carry your satchel."

Although the bag was heavy, Grace kept pace with her mother as they left the school and started up the hill toward the Smiths' home.

"Just what illness does Tommy have, anyway?" she asked her mother. "I hope it's not the flu again."

"Mrs. Smith didn't say why he's been away. As for the flu, Dr. Fred thinks that the epidemic has come and gone and won't be back. I pray he's right."

On the Smiths' doorstep, Grace hung back and let her mother knock. The front window curtain moved, yet no one came. Muffled voices rose inside. Mother rapped again. Then the door opened, and a tired-looking woman stepped out. Mrs. Smith's red hair, escaping its bun, hung in strands around her unsmiling face. Coloured threads clung to her skirt.

"Good afternoon," she said. "Have you brought Tommy's homework?"

"Yes, I have it here," Mother said. "If he isn't too ill, I could go over it with him."

Then someone came up behind Mrs. Smith, a man with red-rimmed eyes in a pale, bearded face.

"Who are you and what do you want?" He sounded angry.

"It's O.K., Uncle Walt." Tommy appeared, and took the man by the arm. "My teacher has brought my homework. Come on, now, and have some tea."

Mrs. Smith stepped outside the house and pulled the door shut.

"Please excuse my brother," she said, her lips trembling. "He hasn't been well."

"I'm sorry," said Mother. "What seems to be the trouble?"

"Shell shock. When he first came back from the war he was very quiet. He sat staring out the window and didn't have much to say. I thought he was just exhausted and that rest and home cooking would soon put him to rights. Walt always was a quiet boy. He *was* a boy when he left, just sixteen. He lied about his age to enlist."

Mother nodded.

"I've always been proud of Walt," Mrs. Smith said, jutting out her jaw. "He heeded the call of King and Empire. He's a hero. But he's been home for two months now and he's in a state. He stares into space. He complains of ringing ears, and he jumps at any loud noise. His nightmares are the worst. He shouts in his sleep, then wakes, sweating, with his heart pounding. He gets up and paces, and won't calm down unless Tommy gets up and sits with him. Tommy has been too tired these last two days to go to school."

"Have you called Dr. Fred?" asked Mother.

Mrs. Smith shook her head.

"I could have a word with Fred and have him stop in."

Mrs. Smith hesitated. "I'm afraid he'll send Walt to an asylum and I don't want that. Walt never shirked his duty; he wasn't a coward on the battlefield. He had plenty of moral fibre."

"I don't doubt that," Mother said. "I'm sure he has seen terrible things that haunt him. Fred is a sympathetic listener. May we come inside and meet your brother properly? Will you introduce us?"

"Of course."

Tears spilled out of Mrs. Smith's eyes. Mother put her arms around her, then lent her a handkerchief.

When they entered, the pale unshaven man was at the table trying to drink his tea. When he lifted his cup to his lips, his hands shook badly so he set it down. He looked up at Mother, Mrs. Smith introduced them and they shook hands.

"I'm glad you've come home," Mother told him. "I'm one of Tommy's teachers."

Tommy, standing behind his uncle, pulled out a chair for Mother. She thanked him.

"Grace, if I may have the grammar book," she said, "I'll show Tommy about parsing sentences."

As Mrs. Smith poured tea for everyone, Mother went over the exercise with Tommy. Grace glanced at the sewing machine in the corner. A white cotton blouse was draped over the back of a chair. She wished it were hers, but, like the youngsters in *The Railway Children*, she wasn't getting any new clothes.

Turning back to the table, she sipped her strong tea and noticed that Tommy was getting the hang of the parts of a sentence. What's more, his uncle was looking on with interest.

"I got As in English grammar," Walt said suddenly.

"Did you? That's grand," said Mother. "Tommy, you're in luck. Your uncle can help you if you get stuck."

As they finished their tea, the adults talked about the weather and the fruit crop. Then Mrs. Smith and Tommy saw them to the door.

"Thank you for the tea. I'll speak to Fred," Mother said softly.

Mrs. Smith mouthed, "Thank you."

"See you at school, Grace." Tommy said.

"For sure," she replied. For the first time in months he'd spoken a civil word to her.

When they were out of earshot, Grace asked her mother what shell shock was.

"An injury to the mind," said Mother. "Lots of soldiers get it. You can't send men off to war, stick them in rat-infested trenches, with guns booming and shells exploding all around them, and their comrades dying beside them, and then expect them to be normal when they come home."

Grace's eyes filled with tears.

"Will he get better?" she asked.

"I hope so, in time. Maybe Uncle Fred will have some ideas."

Grace trudged along, deep in thought.

"You know the co-op store that Uncle Fred and some of the Finnish families are organizing?" she remarked. "Maybe, when it's started, Walt could work there. There shouldn't be too many loud noises in a store."

"That's a good idea. I'll mention it to Fred."

At home, Grace went up the outside stairs while Mother entered the house by the front door to see if the doctor was in.

CHAPTER FIFTEEN

"It's your turn to peel the potatoes," Charles informed Grace the following day when they got home from school. Checking the schedule posted on the kitchen wall, she saw that, sure enough, it was. Below the schedule of chores was a list of towns and dates, indicating where Father would be on any given day of his lecture tour. Grace scowled at it, then went to get out the potatoes and paring knife.

"A lot of good it does, knowing where he is," she thought as she peeled. Sure, it was good to know where he could be reached in an emergency, but there was no emergency, just the daily grind. Father had all the fun of travelling and meeting people who were glad to see him, while the rest of the family was stuck with school and chores, and making do, and doing without. Sometimes she wished they had a normal family life with a father who left for work every morning and came home every evening.

Mother's near-firing from her teaching position had made clear to Grace the way her father's principles made things hard for the family. She wished she could talk about her bad feelings to someone. As she put the potatoes in water, she looked out the window and saw that the rain that had been threatening was pouring down. There was no point in asking Kathy to go for a walk. Besides, she wouldn't share her unhappy thoughts about Father with Kathy. Because Father's enemies said so many unkind things about him, she would never say a word against him outside the family circle.

She made up her mind to talk to Mother about her concerns, but waited until the evening meal was over and the younger children were in bed. Howard took a long time to settle down, and, as Mother sang to him to get him to sleep, Grace read the newspaper at the kitchen table.

It was dated May 13th, 1919, three days ago. She unfolded it and spread it out, wondering if there might be any mention of Father's speaking tour. Skipping the story about the Paris peace talks, she was drawn to a headline: "*Labour Unrest in Winnipeg.*"

Her eyes scanned the page. Talks between the workers in the building and metal trades and their employers had broken down. The workers wanted higher wages and better working conditions and had appealed for help to the Winnipeg Trades and Labour Council, an umbrella organization of all the unions. The Trades and Labour Council made a public statement that if the employers wouldn't meet the workers' demands, it would call upon all its member unions to strike in sympathy with them. Seventy other unions had also voted to walk out in support. If the

Trades and Labour Council should call for a strike, Winnipeg would grind to a halt.

Grace looked up as her mother came out of the bedroom with the usual pile of mending. She sat at the table and heaved a sigh.

"The baby is finally asleep," she said.

"Have you read the paper?" Grace asked her.

"I haven't had time. Tell me what's in it."

Mother threaded her needle and picked up Ralph's trousers, which needed patches on the knees. Grace filled her in.

"The editorial says that if there's a general strike in Winnipeg it will be the first step in a Bolshevik Revolution like the one in Russia in November 1917."

"I don't believe that," said Mother. "It's about wages."

"The situation sounds scary," Grace remarked. "And Father is God-knows-where."

Mother winced. "Don't take the Lord's name in vain. If you want to know where Father is, look at his itinerary. I believe he's still in British Columbia, up north."

Grace trembled. Here was a chance to talk about what was on her mind.

"Mother, the other night when you were at that school meeting, I was there too."

Mother dropped her mending and stared at Grace.

"Really! I sensed that somebody was at the back of the room in the shadows, but thought it was the caretaker being nosy. So it was you! Grace, I'm disappointed in you. You shouldn't have been eavesdropping. You shouldn't have been out at night, you should have stayed to look after the younger children, as I asked, and you shouldn't concern yourself with grown-up business."

"Kathy was with me, and Belva was here with the children. She was worried about you, wishing Father were with you at the meeting, so I went to see what was happening."

Mother sighed. "Then you saw that I'm a capable person who can handle these problems by herself."

Grace took a deep breath.

"Well, Mother, speaking as your right-hand girl, it seems to me that you have too much work and not enough money. I've thought a lot about things, and to be honest, I blame Father."

Mother's eyes widened. "You do?"

"Yes. I love it here at the Landing but I wish our family life was different."

"In what way?"

"Well, for one thing, I wish he were home more."

"But many fathers work away from home. Anna's dad is away at the sawmill all week."

"Yes," said Grace, "but Mr. Kangas comes home on weekends and is good company for Anna and her mother and sisters. He sings funny songs in Finnish when he's tipsy."

Mother's eyes flashed.

"I suppose you'd be happier," she said, her voice dangerously low, "if your father were a drunkard in a ditch."

"Of course not!" Grace exclaimed. "And Mr. Kangas isn't a drunkard in a ditch. He just likes a little nip to take the edge off things after a hard week. All I'm asking is for you to persuade Father to find a normal job and be here more. He's always away, and when he does come home he's tired and we have to be quiet and let him rest. And he's always telling us to be tidy, speak correctly and do our chores promptly. We're doing the best we can. It's not as if he's here every day, lending a helping hand."

Mother's lips trembled.

"You're not being fair, Grace. Many fathers got killed in the war. Be glad yours is alive. As for him instructing you when he is home, well, that's what a good parent does. You children get too used to me and my easy-going ways. I'm glad when your father makes you pull up your socks."

Grace paused. "Well, maybe that's good. But that's not all I have to say. We as a family never know what's coming next. Our lives change drastically whenever Father's work changes. I love it here at the Landing, but I also liked our life in the North End of Winnipeg when he was at the Stella Avenue Mission."

Mother smiled. "I liked our life there too. There was such a happy feeling at the mission. All the different languages that people spoke made me think of a magical woodland full of birds."

She began reminiscing about the newcomers to Canada who came to classes in English, nutrition, and child care, and to enjoy the gymnasium with the swimming pool. Sometimes young women who had come to the mission stayed with Grace's family for a few months, where they did light housekeeping and helped with the younger children until they left to have babies of their own.

"We had so many interesting visitors," Mother said. "Do you remember the man who headed a religious community that was vegetarian? I explained to you when you were a little girl that they believed that it was wrong to kill anything, even for food. You said, *'What about mosquitoes? Is it wrong to kill them even if they are very thick?'*"

Grace laughed, but she knew Mother was diverting her attention, leading her down memory lane, hoping she'd forget what was on her mind.

"We were talking about Father," she said.

Her mother sighed.

"So we were. All his life your father has been searching for the best ways to serve humanity. When the war came he felt he had to take a stand."

"Fine, but when Father takes a stand it affects us all. I don't mind our shabby clothes, but I get tired of always being in the minority, and of people not liking us, like those men at the school the other night."

"Plenty of people like and respect us."

"Maybe. But we at home are getting the short end of the stick. Here we are, worrying about Father, wishing he were home, and meanwhile he's probably addressing an audience and receiving wild applause. I think he feels a thrill, like we kids when we try something daring. Does he stop to think of us at all?"

Mother looked stern.

"You know, Grace, if your father and I were a different type of parent, we would be angry at you for questioning our judgment. Most parents wouldn't put up with the tone you're taking. It's disrespectful."

Grace's lips started to tremble.

"But we believe in explaining things to you children," Mother continued in the quiet voice that she used when she was upset. "Now, to answer your question, yes, your father does miss you and the others. Let me read you something."

Wearily she rose and went into her bedroom. She returned with a letter.

"Your father wrote me this four years ago, back in November 1915 when he was on a speaking tour with the Bureau of Social Research. He was in Montreal at the time."

Mother unfolded the paper and began to read.

It's wonderful that you and I can be together in this work. I felt yesterday you were right when you said that we shouldn't give up yet. So when I get discouraged, you have to keep me going. Mr. D has two beautiful children. His little girl of nine is a very lovable child. I felt hungry for our own little ones."

Mother had tears in her eyes.

"So you see, he does miss you and your brothers and sister. Furthermore, I'm the one who tells him not to give up. I agree one hundred per cent with what he's doing. When you children get older, I intend to be more actively involved in the peace movement, but right now you need me here at home."

"I don't know what we'd do without you!" blurted Grace. "But you work so hard!"

"But I love being in the classroom again, using my education and earning a bit of money to help support us. Now, please go to bed and sleep, and trust me and your father a little more."

Grace kissed her mother goodnight and went to bed, but lay awake for some time. Mother's strong and cheerful attitude encouraged her, but still, she had a feeling that something bad might happen.

CHAPTER SIXTEEN

A letter came from Auntie in Winnipeg. Mother read it, frowning, then put it up on the kitchen shelf out of reach of the younger children. After the evening meal, when the boys were washing the dishes and Grace and Belva were in the living room doing their homework, she came through with the letter on top of the clean laundry in the basket.

"You two are the oldest," she said softly, "and I think you should read Auntie's news. But don't discuss it with the others. They're too little and it would only worry them."

Grace seized the letter, and she and Belva put their heads together over the pages of Auntie's neat, slanted script. First Auntie hoped they were all in good health and said that "Mama" (that was Grandmother) was well, though suffering some aches and pains of old age. Then came the political news.

"We had a letter today from James saying that his speaking tour will bring him to Winnipeg on June 8th. Knowing James, I am sure he will want to get involved in the

conflict that has divided this city and threatens to bring it to a standstill. We here at home wish he would avoid the trouble that is brewing. If you have any means of communicating with him, Lucy, would you beg him to change his plans and linger awhile in the other western provinces?

"As you know, this time last year we narrowly avoided a general strike here in Winnipeg. It didn't happen, because both the provincial and the federal governments told the Winnipeg mayor and city council to reach a settlement with the workers. Since the war was still going on, then, governments didn't want any disruption of the war effort.

"Now we're on the brink of a general strike, again. In the metal fabrications industry the bosses and managers are hostile to the machinists, who want a wage increase and the right to bargain collectively, as a union. The city employees, too, such as the electrical workers, the firemen and police, and the men who drive the teams of horses that pull city carts and wagons, want the same thing. A lot of soldiers have returned from the war and are looking for good jobs with a decent wage, and support the machinists and the city employees.

"Everything costs more than it did last year. And after the terrible flu that swept through last winter, bringing so many deaths, people have been upset, short-tempered and looking for a fight. They are critical of the prime minister ruling like a king through orders-in-council.

"You and James know all this, of course, but you may not realize how tense things are in Winnipeg right now. A couple of days ago the mayor and the provincial premier had an emergency conference, but failed to arrange talks between themselves and the Strike Committee. Meanwhile, people are stocking up on supplies. I went out the other day and bought staples like flour and sugar. I hear that the city police voted to

go on strike but that the leaders of the Strike Committee asked that they remain on duty, so that the city won't be put under martial law.

"If 25,000 to 30,000 workers walk off their jobs, as they likely will on May 15th, we'll get no mail, have no street cars, no telephone or telegram service, and possibly no milk or bread deliveries, though I hear that the Strike Committee plans to give its permission for this sort of essential service to keep running.

"The printers and others that work for Mr. Dafoe at the Winnipeg Free Press will go on strike in sympathy, but the Rev. William Ivens, I understand, is going to publish a newspaper with volunteer help, one which will keep the public informed of developments, from the strikers' point of view.

"Like everyone else in our family, I sympathise with the demand for decent wages and working conditions and the right to form a union and bargain as a group. But when some of our neighbours here in the south end are getting out their muskets and burying their valuables in the garden, it makes me nervous. The Winnipeg Free Press is doing its best to whip up fear; they say that a strike will be the start of a Russian-style revolution.

"If you can, please keep James away from Winnipeg at this dangerous time. I admire his urge to help others and his bravery in standing up for what is right. You have been wonderful, going along with all his career changes, and now you're teaching school to help make ends meet. But your little family has been through enough already, so if you can, please keep James out of this volatile situation. I enclose a small gift of money for the children."

Then Auntie wrote "Love", and signed her name.

Mother, who was back from putting away the clean clothes, found Belva trembling, while Grace re-read the letter.

"There's no way of telling Father not to go, is there?" Belva quavered.

Mother shook her head. "No, and he will want to be there. The strike leaders, like Mr. Dixon and Mr. Ivens, are his friends and colleagues."

Belva uttered a sob. Grace grabbed her hand and held it.

"Don't upset yourself, Belva. Father will be all right."

Grace spoke more confidently than she felt, but it wasn't helpful to stir up fear among the younger children.

"I think Auntie is being a worry-wart, don't you, Mother?" she added. "I can just picture Father on a platform addressing a big crowd, and explaining workers' rights to them, and getting a huge round of applause, can't you?"

Mother nodded. Then she muttered "Excuse me," and rushed back into the bedroom.

Grace's heart sank. She suspected that her mother was crying. She turned to Belva.

"Let's go to the kitchen and put the dishes away. Charles can't reach the high shelves."

After supper, Kathy knocked on the door and asked Grace if she'd like to go for a walk on the beach. Grace said yes. As they strolled down the hill, she told Kathy about her aunt's letter.

"Maybe your dad will be able to talk to both sides and help them reach an agreement before a strike breaks out," Kathy said.

"Maybe."

Gulls hovered overhead, always hopeful for a meal. The girls sat in silence for a while on a log that had rolled in on the tides. Then Kathy rose and walked some distance away to a tidepool carved out of the rocks. Grace joined her. Tidepools always contained interesting marine life, like tiny crabs and starfish. The little wet world fascinated the girls, and they sat and stared at it, losing track of time. Then they decided to continue their stroll. All sorts of sea life were strewn on the beach. Long ropes of seaweed, barnacles, mussels, more crabs. On a dock a youth watched his fishing line bob in the water.

Suddenly Kathy stooped. "Look!" she exclaimed, picking up a frosted jade green oblong of glass. "This must be from a whisky bottle."

Before coming to the Landing, Grace hadn't known there was such a thing as sea glass. She'd learned that the best time to look for it was at low tide after a storm. It was ordinary glass that got into the sea, and was tumbled and ground until the sharp edges were smoothed and rounded.

"It's beautiful," she said. Once, soon after they'd moved to the Landing, she'd found a piece of amber coloured glass, probably from a medicine bottle, and had given it to her mother. Mother said she would get it made into a pendant some day and kept it in her top bureau drawer beside her Bible.

"You can have this piece." Kathy held it out to her. "I have some at home."

"Really? Thank you. I love the colour." Grace held the glass up to the light. The green glass had an almost powdery texture. It wasn't transparent.

Out of nowhere she remembered a Bible passage from Sunday School days, about the need to have faith, hope and love: *"For now we see through a glass darkly; but then, face to face; now I know in part, but then shall I know even as also I am known."*

The oval of glass, translucent but not transparent, was like her situation. She had no way of seeing what was happening to Father in the world beyond the mountains. She was doing her best to understand the struggles going on, but she knew only in part. Maybe the sea glass was a sign that she'd understand it all by and by.

"Keep it," Kathy urged. "Get it made into a pendant someday."

"Thank you, Kathy," Grace said. "You're a good friend."

CHAPTER SEVENTEEN

On May 15th the Winnipeg machinists and building trade workers went on strike, and other trade unionists walked off their jobs in support. That day, a letter arrived from Father. When Charles brought it home, just before their evening meal, and handed it to Mother, she took it into the bedroom to read. Usually she opened family letters in front of everyone and read parts of them aloud. Grace called the younger children to the table and served the fish chowder. A few minutes later Mother came out to the kitchen and sat down at the head of the table. She cleared her throat.

"You older children have heard about the general strike in Winnipeg," she began. "Your father wrote this letter while on the train between Prince Rupert and Edmonton. He said he was going to Winnipeg in the hope of bringing the two sides to an agreement, before the workers walk out."

"But it's too late," murmured Belva.

"What's a strike?" asked five year old Bruce.

Charles's eyes twinkled. "It's when you are up to bat and you don't hit the ball. Three strikes and you're out."

"Now, Charles, tell him properly." Mother took a sip of water. "Charles is talking about a strike in baseball," she told the little boy, "but this is a different kind of strike."

"O.K." said Charles. "It's when the men who work at a factory say to the bosses: *Our work is hard and our workplace is dangerous and we don't get enough money. We want you to fix up the place we work in and pay us a fair wage. If you don't, we're going to stop the machines or lay down our tools and walk out. And we're going to march with picket signs outside the factory until you change your mind.*"

"It's not quite like that," Grace said. "It can be at any work place, not just a factory, and it's not just men who are workers. The Winnipeg telephone operators are mostly girls and they've gone out in support of the machinists and the building trade workers."

"If they don't go to work, who will pay them?" Ralph piped up.

"That's a good question. Who knows the answer?" Mother looked around the table.

Charles shrugged and helped himself to some bread and butter.

"The strikers have to live on their savings, if they have any," Belva offered.

"That's right." Grace chipped in. "Also, the machinists' and building trade workers' unions will have saved some money and received donations from other workers in sympathy with them. If there's a strike, the unions will pay some of this money to each striker."

"What if they run out?" asked Charles.

"Then they'll have to go back to work and take whatever their employers are willing to pay them," Mother told him, "and that would mean they'd lost the struggle. That's why it's important to plan ahead for a strike and call one only if there's enough money to hold out for a long time."

"But a strike would be hard on the factory owners, too," Grace said. "The bosses would be losing money, because there would be no one to make the machine parts or whatever it is that the company sells."

"That's what the strikers count on," Mother said. "Now, who wants more chowder?"

Charles smiled. "If we don't get more soup we'll go on strike."

Howard banged his spoon, and the little boys chanted, "We want soup!" as the others laughed, except for Grace.

To her, the strike was no laughing matter, and this feeling was reinforced when she went down to get the newspapers that Uncle Fred had saved for her family. The *Toronto Star* reported that the strike was not a Bolshevik revolution, but rather, a strike over wages, working conditions, and the right to collective bargaining. That was what Mother said and it sounded true to Grace. Father would never support any violent action to overthrow the government. He believed in changing governments through the ballot box.

Another newspaper story was about a big outdoor meeting in Winnipeg's Victoria Park, attended by 1,000 striking workers. The speakers' names were listed. Grace ran her finger along the list, and near the end was Father.

She read in another article that two new laws had just been passed by the federal government in Ottawa. The Immigration Act had been changed, and now "undesirables" could be shipped out of Canada to their country of origin without a hearing. Also, an addition had been made to the Criminal Code. This new section, 98, permitted people to be arrested on suspicion of a crime. It was up to the accused person to prove his innocence, instead of the other way around. Grace bit her lip. She would have to ask Mother to explain exactly what it meant, but it didn't sound fair.

In the *Western Labour News* she found an article by Father. Grace read it carefully. In talking about the inconvenience that a strike would pose for everyday Winnipeggers, Father asked, "Why blame the strikers? Why not blame the employers whose arrogant determination has provoked the strike?"

Grace shivered. He was really in the thick of things now.

Over the next few days, she acted as if everything were normal, but she couldn't get Father and Winnipeg off her mind. News came from Vancouver and other B.C. towns about workers walking off their jobs in sympathy with the strikers in Winnipeg. On May 30, three hundred workers in Prince Rupert walked out. In Vancouver the employees of the *Daily Sun* shut the newspaper down because they didn't like the anti-strike editorials.

Uncle Fred went to Vancouver and came home excited about the widespread support for the Winnipeg strike. When he sat on the porch to read, the older children gathered around him and peppered him with questions.

"What's the latest in Winnipeg?" Grace began.

"Something amazing is going on there," said the doctor. "It's remarkable to have the entire work force of a major city close it down. To have a workers' Strike Committee deciding what essential services will be provided is new and radical. What's happening in Winnipeg is historic. The strike is no longer about higher wages and the right to collective bargaining. It's an experiment in direct democracy."

Uncle Fred was waving his hands for emphasis. He was in full oratorical flight.

"You girls will be interested that Helen Armstrong, head of the Women's Labour League, has led the way in setting up a restaurant in the Strathcona Hotel where they offer meals to strikers. Everyone is invited to come and eat there, and pay only what they can afford. They have a sign on the wall that says, *No one need want*."

He turned to Grace, Belva and Kathy.

"You girls know that the telephone operators – women – were the first to go out in sympathy with the metal and construction workers. The next to go out were the bakery and confectionery workers, again mostly women, not in a union, yet willing to risk their jobs to show their support for the strikers. And gangs of women have been blocking delivery trucks from the big department stores, because the drivers aren't out on strike. The women in the Weston area of Winnipeg did something even more drastic. You probably know where Weston is."

"Near the CPR shops," Grace murmured.

"Well, a group of women from Weston went to their local firehall and physically removed the scabs – the young men from the Citizens' Committee – who came in to do the work of the striking fire fighters."

Uncle Fred's eyes flashed with excitement.

"What's a scab?" asked Charles.

Dr. Fred hesitated.

"It's an insulting name that striking workers use for replacement workers who take over their jobs. Don't use it lightly. In Winnipeg the city is being run by the Strike Committee, made up of trade union representatives. They're seeing that essential services are provided, like bread and milk deliveries. But there's also a Citizens' Committee made up of businessmen and company owners who are against the strikers. They don't like the Strike Committee running the city, so they've got men volunteering to take over some of the services; in other words, to scab."

He paused, then thought of something more.

"These replacement workers in the firehalls are being run ragged," he added. "Seems there have been a lot of fire alarms, often in the middle of the night. The firefighters hop in the firetrucks and go out to answer the call, and often it turns out to be a false alarm."

Charles grinned. "It's the strikers and their supporters who are setting off these false alarms, isn't it, to keep the scabs in the firehalls busy?"

As Uncle Fred nodded, Grace bit her lip. The scene in Winnipeg sounded frightening. She couldn't imagine herself blocking delivery trucks or dragging replacement workers out of fire stations. If only the employers would go back to the bargaining table with the metal and construction workers, and give them higher wages and the right to form unions. Then they'd go back to work, and Father could come home.

In the days that followed, the news got worse. The Royal North West Mounted Police came at night to the strike leaders' homes, arrested them and took them off to jail. Among those arrested was Father's friend, the Reverend William Ivens of the Labour Church. Mother learned this from the school inspector who had come over from Vancouver. After Mr Ivens' arrest, there was no one to edit the strikers' newspaper, so Father and Fred Dixon, a Member of the Manitoba legislature, stepped up, with Father acting as editor and Mr. Dixon as reporter.

Rumour had it that the strike leaders were going to be deported to Britain without being tried in a Canadian court, but Dr. Fred didn't think that would happen. Instead, he thought that the authorities would try them in Winnipeg, to show what could happen if you defied the rich and powerful.

Grace was shocked to learn that among those arrested were two city aldermen, John Queen and Abraham Heaps. These men had been voted into office by citizens.

Then came news of "Bloody Saturday" – the name the newspapers gave to June 21st, 1919. With the adults, Grace pored over the papers and discussed the accounts of what had happened. As far as she could figure out, returned soldiers who understood the strikers' situation and hoped to find decent-paying jobs, planned a silent, peaceful march in support of the strike. The Winnipeg police, who had sympathized with the strikers, had been asked by the Strike Committee to stay on the job and keep order. Then the Winnipeg city government fired the police who sympathized with the strike, and replaced them by special police. In Uncle Fred's opinion, these "specials" were armed thugs, intent on union-busting.

The soldiers' march in support of the strikers turned into a big parade with many people, including striking workers, joining the war veterans. A scuffle broke out, and then the special police, mounted on horses, charged into the crowd swinging heavy cudgels. Then, out came soldiers armed with machine guns, and the parade was broken up in front of city hall. A messenger boy was killed, and a hundred other people were injured.

Reading about it, Grace started to shake. Where was Father?

That night she couldn't sleep. She got up and found her mother at the kitchen table.

"Mother?" she began. Her mother got up and took her in her arms. Then she pulled out a chair for her and got her some milk.

"I know you're worried," she said. "So am I. But your father wouldn't want to be anywhere else but Winnipeg at this time. He's prepared for whatever happens."

"But what about us?"

Mother stroked her hair.

"I'll look after you. Your father knows this. We've been through trouble before."

"It's bad, not knowing where he is or what's happening." Grace wiped her eyes on the sleeve of her nightgown.

"Your father has a safe haven to go to, your grandmother's house," Mother told her.

"But what if they arrest him before he can go there?"

"Then he's with the other strike leaders, in good company."

"May I stay home school tomorrow in case there's news?"

Mother shook her head.

"If any news comes to the house, Aunt Alice has promised to send me a note. Tomorrow we're going to school as usual."

CHAPTER EIGHTEEN

At school the next morning it was hard to concentrate, and Grace was glad when lunch time came. She, Anna and Kathy sat under the arbutus tree with their lunch pails. On purpose, Grace turned the conversation to the principles of geometry, which they would need to know for the exams. Anna was quoting the rule about the square on the hypotenuse when Grace saw Belva coming toward them. Her sister's doleful face told her that news had come and it wasn't good.

"Excuse me." She sprang up and ran to join her sister.

"Mother wants you." Then they saw their mother coming out of the elementary school building, where she taught the Entrance class.

"Grace, it's as we feared," she said, when they reached her side. "Your father has been arrested."

Grace felt as if her knees would buckle. Yet, oddly, at the same time, she was relieved. Waiting had been hard. Mother was being very calm, so Grace straightened her shoulders.

"Well, at least now we know," she said.

Anna and Kathy joined them, and her mother told them the news.

"I'm sorry." Kathy seized one of Grace's hands, and Anna took the other, but only for a moment, because the bell was summoning them to afternoon classes. Mother stood tall and walked back into school, and Grace and Belva followed her example.

That afternoon, Mother taught French as if nothing was wrong. As she worked through a grammar exercise, Grace dreaded the stares, whispers and comments she would face when word got out.

Halfway through French class someone knocked on the door. She looked up and saw Charles. Mother went to the door to talk to him. His teacher thought Mother had accidentally picked up her math text by mistake, and had sent him to fetch it. Mother searched her satchel, found the book for Charles and whispered something to him.

His eyes flashed.

"In jail?" His whisper was audible. "I hope he knocked some scab's teeth in."

"We'll talk at home," Mother murmured. "Off you go, now."

Charles left with a spring to his step.

It seemed to Grace that the school day would never end. From French, Mother moved on to British history, then drawing. At 3:30 she had an extra session with the

Entrance class, which included Belva. Grace set out for home alone, hoping she wouldn't meet anyone. She could imagine someone pointing and saying, "Her father is in jail."

She heard running feet behind her, and turned. Kathy and Anna were pursuing her.

"Listen, don't look so down in the mouth," Anna coaxed. "There's no reason to be embarrassed. Lots of men get put in the pokey. At least your dad is in jail for something important, not for being drunk and disorderly."

"You should be excited," declared Kathy. "This may be the beginning of a revolution in Canada and your father is lucky to be a part of it. My dad envies him."

Neither comment made Grace feel any better, but she managed to thank her friends.

"You should do something to take your mind off your troubles," Anna said. "Come to my house and let my sisters practise their English with you. Mami made a cake."

"Thanks, but I should go home," said Grace.

They walked in silence until Anna turned onto the road that led her home, leaving Kathy and Grace alone.

"This afternoon, let's get Mama to play the organ for us – something cheerful, like *Alexander's Ragtime Band*," Kathy suggested.

"Thanks, but I have chores."

As Grace climbed the outer stairs to their apartment, Ralph met her with a tear-streaked face.

"They say Father's in jail," he blurted. "Is that because he spoke out against the guv-ment?"

The way he said "government" made Grace smile.

She bent and hugged her brother. "Mother will explain it all when she gets home."

Mrs. Erola, who babysat and did light housekeeping for the family, rose from the kitchen table where she had been cutting up vegetables for a stew. She wiped her hands on her apron, then threw her arms around Grace.

"It's a real shame about your father," she murmured.

Shame. The word was like a thud. Grace knew that Mrs. Erola wasn't telling her to be ashamed, but deep inside, she did feel a little bit of shame. In her family, three generations of men had been Methodist ministers. Her grandfather and great-grandfather had never been put behind bars. As caring men of God, they'd been concerned for unfortunates who were in conflict with the law, and had tried to help such people sort out their troubled lives. Grandfather and Great-grandfather must be turning over their graves if they knew Father was in jail.

Or maybe not. Many people in jail were not criminals. People got imprisoned by mistake, or when falsely accused, like the dad in *The Railway Children*. In the Bible, many prophets and disciples were incarcerated and punished for what they stood for. And Jesus got in trouble with the authorities of his day, too.

Grace took Ralph's hand in hers and smiled at Mrs. Erola.

"Father will be all right." She spoke with conviction, as if saying so could make it so. "I'm here now, so if you want to leave early, I can mind the kids and cook the stew."

"All right, dearie," said Mrs. Erola, taking off her apron. "But tell your mami that if I can be of help, to call me."

"Thank you so much."

Grace was glad that Howard was still asleep. Ralph and Bruce were upset, and full of questions, and she didn't have the answers. What if Father was beaten and bleeding? What if he was sent to prison for a long time? She turned to Ralph and Bruce.

"Ralph, do you know what would make me feel better? A story. I'd love it if you would read to me while I finish the stew."

Ralph looked pleased, and Bruce was always eager for a story. By the time Mother, Belva and Charles arrived home around 4:30, Grace had heard three stories, "The Little Red Hen", "The Gingerbread Man" and "Little Red Riding Hood". The stew was bubbling on the stove, the bread was buttered, and Mrs. Erola's cinnamon rolls were on a plate, covered with a clean tea towel.

Nobody felt very hungry, though. Charles kept looking up hesitantly, as if wanting to ask a question but not sure if he should.

Finally Howard, who was beside Mother, put his hand on her arm.

"Smile," he ordered.

Mother smiled and stroked his hair. "Eat your bread," she coaxed. "I'll cut it in smaller pieces for you."

"Father's in jail," Bruce announced. "Hellie told me." Hellie was Kathy's little sister.

Then out came Charles's question: "What did Father do, exactly?"

Mother took a deep breath. "We don't know what he's charged with, but it probably has to do with something he wrote in the strikers' newspaper."

"Can you arrest somebody just because you disagree with them?" Charles persisted. "I mean, we all have opinions."

This remark made Mother's face brighten.

"You're right, Charles. We all have opinions, and in a free society we should be able to express them. But in times of crisis, governments sometimes forbid people to say or write things."

"Why?"

"They don't want people to spread fear, or encourage the enemy."

"But the war is over," Charles pointed out.

"I know, but the government is still in a mood to crack down on dissent."

"Father probably knew he might get arrested but he expressed the workers' point of view anyway," Grace interjected.

Mother nodded. "Your father is a brave man. He has the courage of his convictions."

The little boys didn't understand "courage of his convictions" but they knew what brave meant, and they looked happier.

"When will Father be let out of jail?" Belva asked.

"I hope he gets out on bail soon," Mother said.

"What's bail?" asked Ralph.

"It's money you pay so they'll let you out of jail," Charles informed him.

"It's money you pay to show the court that you won't skip town but will show up for your trial," Grace added.

Belva looked stricken. "Suppose the judge finds Father guilty and puts him away for years?"

"We'll cross that bridge when we come to it," Mother said.

"Where will he get the bail money, Mother?" Grace asked. "Will you send it to him? Do you have enough?"

"Your grandma and aunts and uncles in Winnipeg will bail him out, and then later your father and I will repay them," Mother said.

Howard had enough of this gloomy conversation, for he stood up on the seat of his chair and held out his arms to Mother, who took him on her lap.

"I think we should pray," said Ralph.

Tears sprang into Mother's eyes.

"Very well," she said. "Bow your heads. *Dear Lord, we pray for courage to get us through this bad time, and for all the people who are in want, afraid and injured. Help us remember that hearts that are truly united are never really apart. Amen.*"

CHAPTER NINETEEN

That night, when Mother was putting the little boys to bed, the door of the boys' room was open, and Grace overheard Bruce saying that he was going to pray again for Father. Mother listened to his prayers, and after "Amen", said, "Now, I'll tuck you in."

"You know what I wish?" he said.

"No, what?"

"I wish Father had taken Charles's .22 with him."

Belva and Grace exchanged glances. Peace-loving Father would be horrified to hear that he should be "packing heat".

"I kind of agree with Bruce," whispered Grace.

That night she couldn't sleep. After tossing and turning for what seemed like hours, she eased out of bed so that the squeaky springs wouldn't wake Belva, and tiptoed to the kitchen for a drink of water. She hoped to find Mother there, but she wasn't. She glanced at the clock. 12:30 a.m.

Through the open door leading to the staircase and the ground floor of the house, Grace heard faint voices. Mother must be talking with Alice and Fred. She wished they'd included her in the grown-up conversation, as there was so much about her father's predicament that she didn't understand. Even so, the rise and fall of adult voices was reassuring. All three grown-ups were smart and resourceful. They could figure out what should be done, if anything.

The following day, as if in answer to their prayers, a letter came from Father, written from the provincial jail in Winnipeg. Mother read aloud the part where he said, "much love to the children" but later beckoned Grace and Belva into her bedroom and let them read the whole thing.

Father wrote:

"You once said to me that I'd never feel fulfilled until I got myself into a battle. Yesterday I was arrested on charges of seditious libel. I didn't write anything that encouraged the overthrow of the government – though I did quote two passages from Isaiah. The Labour News isn't going to miss an issue, because Will Ivens has been released on bail and is back on the job as editor.

Brother said, when he came to visit, that Mama is not amused by my being here, but others are proud of me. I got a wire from the Federated Labour Party in Vancouver congratulating me on my martyrdom and hoping I deserve it.

They have called me now for the preliminary hearing so I have to go."

"He doesn't sound discouraged," Grace remarked. "He's cheerful."

"I don't want him to get killed like the Christian martyrs we've read about," whispered Belva.

"That won't happen," Grace said firmly. "He'll be out on bail soon."

"What's *seditious libel*?" Belva asked.

"I don't know exactly. Let's get the dictionary."

The two girls looked up "sedition", which was defined as "any action inciting discontent or rebellion against a government." "Libel" meant "defamation by written or printed words or in any form other than spoken words and gestures." Defamation by spoken words and gestures was "slander."

"Father *did* criticize the government," Belva whispered.

Grace frowned. "Criticized, yes, but I don't think he incited rebellion."

"I wish we could do something to help him," Belva mused.

The following morning, when Mrs. Erola arrived, she told Mother that she would like to take the little boys to her house that day. Her daughter was home, visiting, and she wanted to spend time with her. Both women could keep an eye on Bruce and Howard and chat when they were napping. The boys' faces lit up at the proposed change of scene, and Mother said that would be fun for them.

On the way to school, Belva, Charles and Ralph ran ahead with the other children, leaving Mother walking with Grace and Kathy. Several passersby on the road to the school paused and greeted Mother, saying that they'd heard about Father and hoped he was O.K.

"These are crazy times we live in," one man remarked. Mother thanked him for his concern, and they walked on. Then, suddenly, she paused.

"Grace, I've thought of something you can do to help your father," she said. "Kathy, you may be part of it, but you don't have to."

"Oh, but I'd like to. I'd do anything to help Uncle James," Kathy declared.

Grace liked the sound of "do." It would be great to *do* something instead of just waiting for news.

"What is it?" she asked.

"You know your father is charged with seditious libel. When someone is charged with that, the North West Mounted Police sometimes search his home for evidence. I'm afraid the Mounties may come and search our house. We have books about socialism by Marx and Engels and works by people in the British Fabian Society. You know the volumes I mean. The police might seize them as evidence of sedition."

Grace gasped. "Oh, Mother, we aren't going to burn Father's books, are we?"

"Certainly not. Now, here's what I want you to do."

CHAPTER TWENTY

That afternoon, in the middle of a seatwork exercise in French translation, Grace and Kathy quietly slipped out of the classroom. Once off the school grounds, they walked briskly back to Stonehurst. Upstairs, Grace went to the kitchen cupboard, got out the old breadbox, and found the left-over oilcloth from when they'd covered the table. Kathy lined the breadbox with oil cloth and brought it over to Grace, who was kneeling by the book case selecting any volume that might be considered subversive. She placed Karl Marx and Friedrich Engels in the bread box.

"What about this one?" Kathy held up a book by the British artist William Morris.

Grace paused to think.

"It has a red cover, so the police might think it was written by a Red," she decided. "Put it in the breadbox. You do realize, Kathy, that you can't tell anyone what we're doing."

"I'd never tell, though I wish I could. It's exciting."

Grace's heart was beating fast. When the box was full, she arranged the remaining books so that no one would see the gaps. They slipped the breadbox into the burlap bag that the used clothes had come in and took it downstairs. Kathy found a shovel and took the lead, while Grace dragged the heavy sack. They went through the garden behind the house and into the woods.

The trail was narrow and rough, but once they were out of sight of the house, Grace felt more at ease. On a hike last year, Father had remarked that "God breathes in the forests," and today as the wind ruffled her hair she felt that it was so. Vines trailed across the path, brushing their foreheads. From somewhere came the fragrance of mint.

They stopped to rest several times. Finally they came to a green glade where the trees rose high to the sun. There were many fallen logs covered with a carpet of moss like moist sponge, where green berries flecked with wine-coloured speckles sprouted. Lichen trailed like veils from the branches overhead.

"Here." Grace nodded at a great fallen log that was perched up slightly on a stump. They set their burden down, and knelt to dig a cavity underneath it, scooping out brown leaves. They shoved the breadbox in until it could not be seen, then covered up the opening with moss and dead leaves.

"How will you find it again?" Kathy asked.

Grace frowned. "Mark a tree?" She wished she had brought Charles's pocket knife so that she could carve something, like a heart.

"Use my hair ribbon," Kathy offered.

Grace hesitated. Kathy's ribbon was wide and pink.

"It's too beautiful and too obvious," she said. "Anyone who came up here and saw it tied to a branch would guess that it's marking something, and they might start digging and find our secret vault. We'll use my ribbons instead."

She began untying the thin red ribbons at the ends of her braids.

"Secret Vault! That will be our code name for this place!" Kathy exclaimed, as she tied one of Grace's ribbons to a cedar bough. Then she tied both of Grace's braids behind her shoulders with the remaining ribbon.

"If anyone comments on your hair, just say you lost a ribbon," she advised.

"Good idea. Now, Kathy, you go back to school ahead of me, so we don't draw attention to ourselves."

When Kathy disappeared around the bend in the trail, Grace put the shovel inside the burlap bag and started walking at a normal pace, counting her footsteps so that she would know how many it took to the secret vault, just in case the hair ribbon rotted in the rain.

The next important news from the world beyond the mountains was that the general strike had been officially called off on June 26th. The strike leaders had been arrested and strike funds were getting low. The Manitoba government promised a Royal Commission to find out what had led to one death and over one hundred people injured.

A letter arrived from Father, dated June 26, 1919. Mother read aloud from it at supper time. He began by saying that this letter had to be censored, so details would have to be omitted at present. Then he wrote:

"Yesterday I was taken to the police station and though I made no request, was remanded for eight days. You will notice by the papers that a number of the arrested men have been remanded so I suppose that policy is to be adopted generally.

This experience isn't so trying as the first plunge on the waterfront. Conventional standards no longer loom very large with us, do they? The men with me are very decent fellows arrested on Saturday in connection with the riots. Many of them have wives and children. Several are foreigners who don't even understand the charges on which they are held....

In looking back there is nothing that I have done that I regret. My articles were carefully considered. Of course, in the pressure and novelty of working on a paper, something may have found a place that should not, but I don't think so. The fact is that a great fight is on and if one enters it, he must be prepared to face the risks. It's a serious thing to leave a privileged class and join the ranks of common labor. This is all a part of it.

Conditions here might be worse. The guards are considerate. The food is passable. The bed is not unlike Bruce's. Today we had an outing in the yard. By the way, it seems strange to be near to the old Cooper St. home. Last night I got in some books so I can read and rest – that isn't so bad. The confinement isn't really greater than that on a railroad train. Since I don't smoke I don't have the gnawing pains of many and one realizes the meaning of the old saying, "my mind to me a kingdom is."

I presume bail has been applied for and refused. I had decided not to accept bail in any case til the strike was called off.

So now it's simply a case of wait. I'm not worrying in the least. I don't think they can make the charges stick. If so, well then one must face the inevitable as many have had to, down through the ages.

Tell the children what we have tried to tell them from time to time. I'm sure they will all try to help you out during the holidays. Before long I'll arrange to have some money sent. Write your people. This will work out for the best.

Hope you will all have a happy summer now that the holidays have come.

With much love to each.

Yours, James.

"Hurrah!" shouted Charles. "He may be in jail but he won't let it get him down."

The children looked at each other.

"I guess when he sent this he didn't know that the strike is over," Belva remarked.

"Well, I feel better!" declared Grace. It was true. She had a feeling of accomplishment after hiding the books. "If Father believes things will work out for the best, we should take his word for it."

Though she didn't feel as positive as she sounded, she was pleased to see her little brothers' faces relax.

"Mother, I will help you out in the holidays," Ralph piped up solemnly.

There was a chorus of "Me too."

"I know you will, my little shavers," said Mother, "and we'll be happy because your father wants us to."

A few days later another letter came from Father, out on bail. The little kids thought he would be home soon, but Grace knew better. At some point, he would have to stand trial in Winnipeg, and no one knew yet when that would be. Father wrote that he'd kept the tin spoon they'd given him in jail as a souvenir. Two days after his release, Mr. Ivens' Labour Church had an evening service outside the city limits which was well attended, and Father spoke from the platform to raise money for the men still behind bars.

The next task, he said, was for the labour movement to raise money to pay the lawyer who would defend the strike leaders when they went to trial. Another important task was to present the strikers' side of the matter to the people of Canada. Though the strike failed, the very fact that it had taken place was an inspiration to many Canadians. Father had agreed to travel as far east as Montreal, addressing public meetings in towns along the way, telling people about his arrest, about Bloody Sunday and the labour movement's vision of a fairer, more equal society.

After reading this last sentence, Mother looked up and saw six long faces.

"I sure wish he was coming home now," Charles said, and the younger ones nodded agreement.

"He'll come back as soon as he can," Mother told them, rising to put the letter up in the cupboard. "In the meantime, you can work on your drawings and stories for Father's Book."

Grace was disappointed, because she wanted to tell Father in person about the secret vault. It didn't seem a wise thing to put in a letter.

Later, when the others were in bed and Mother was downstairs talking to Fred and Alice, Grace took down Father's most recent letter. When she read the ending, intended for Mother alone, she felt like an intruder. Ashamed that she had ever questioned her mother about her love for Father, she quickly returned it to the shelf.

"I miss you badly, my darling," he wrote. *"Without your support and encouragement I would never have had the courage to go out on a limb so many times. It means everything to me that we are of one mind about the need to work for a better world. All my love. James."*

*

"Grace, how was your week?"

The family was gathered around the table, and as usual, Mother was encouraging everyone to participate in a conversation. The little boys had fun at Mrs. Erola's the other day. Ralph got 100% on his arithmetic test. Belva said she'd been nervous about her entrance exams but much relieved that Father was all right. Charles announced that he wanted to learn the violin.

"Why the sudden interest?" asked Mother.

Charles explained that he'd heard Aunt Alice playing a recording on the Victrola by a famous violinist, Efrem Zimbalist, who sounded amazing. He wanted to play like him. Ralph said that he too would like to learn.

"We'll see," said Mother. "Now, Grace, it's your turn. tell us your thoughts."

"Well, like everyone else, I'm tremendously happy that Father is O.K.," she said. "And Kathy and I have a project for this summer. We're going to write a novel."

"More Indian legends?" asked Mother.

She shook her head.

"A novel like *The Railway Children*?" asked Belva.

"A little like that. We're calling it *The Mystery of the Secret Vault*." She met Mother's eyes. A knowing flicker passed between them.

"What an intriguing title!" she said.

"You'll never get around to it," said Charles "You'll be having too much fun outdoors."

"Now, don't discourage your sister," said Mother. She had made it clear that she didn't want to know the specific location of the hiding place, so that if the police asked her where her husband's books were, she wouldn't have to lie.

"Grace's cheeks are flushed," Charles remarked."I'll bet she's wearing rouge."

"She's a painted lady," said Ralph.

"I am not!" Grace pretended to be offended. It was a relief to be able to joke again.

Life at the Landing was good that summer. Grace turned fourteen on July 25th. The Royal North West Mounted Police never showed up to search for Father's books, but Grace and Kathy agreed that they had better leave them in the secret vault until they knew the outcome of Father's trial. The novel, of course, was never begun; it had been Grace's way of signalling to Mother that they had hidden the books.

Belva was happy that summer. She and Tommy Smith tied for first in the Entrance class, and both were very proud. She and his mother struck up a conversation about sewing one day when they met on Marine Drive and as a result, Mrs. Smith helped her make a new white blouse.

One day Mother took all of the children to Vancouver to the dentist, and while there, she bought Charles and Ralph a second hand violin and arranged for them to have lessons. "It's not a Stradivarius," she remarked, "but it will serve its purpose."

That summer, Charles often went fishing with Uncle Fred's boys, Tommy Smith, and Tommy's Uncle Walt. Walt often came over and spent an evening talking with Uncle Fred, when the doctor was free. All of the children went swimming and digging clams, and enjoyed beach picnics. Grace and Kathy sometimes referred mysteriously to the S.V., meaning "Secret Vault", but never breathed a word that they had hidden Father's books.

That summer, both girls bought "Workers' Liberty Bonds." The Defence Committee for the jailed strike leaders were encouraging people to buy them, having got the idea from the government's practice of selling "war bonds" to the public to fund the war. The "Workers' Liberty Bonds" were not redeemable and wouldn't increase in value; they were just a fund-raising idea. People bought them to show their support for collective bargaining and fair wages that kept up with inflation. They were available in denominations as low as one dollar and Grace wanted one as a souvenir.

The Defence Committee also published a pamphlet of Father's and Fred Dixon's articles that had appeared in the labour paper at the time of the strike. Grace pored over it, particularly the article that had gotten Father into trouble. In it he'd quoted from the Bible, the prophet, Isaiah:

"Woe unto them that decree unrighteous decrees, and that write grievousness which they have prescribed, to turn aside the needy from judgment, and take away the right of the poor of my people, that widows may be their prey and that they may rob the fatherless." (Isaiah 10:1-2)

"And they shall build houses and inhabit them, and they shall plant vineyards and eat the fruit of them. They shall not build and another inhabit; they shall not plant and another eat, for as the days of a tree are the days of my people, and mine elect shall long enjoy the work of their hands." (Isaiah 65: 21-22)

As far as Grace could see, these verses warned lawmakers to be fair, and spoke of the right of working people to enjoy the fruits of their labour.

Also in the pamphlet was a copy of the open letter from Father to the leading businessmen of Winnipeg, urging them to meet with the strike leaders to try to reach a settlement. The grown-ups agreed with her that these quotes and writings weren't seditious or libellous.

Father wrote home regularly. He said that two of the accused, Winnipeg Alderman Abraham Heaps, and Mr. Fred Dixon, intended to conduct their own defence rather than have a lawyer represent them in court. Father had thought of doing the same thing, but the lawyer hired by the Defence Committee advised him not to. The attorney was afraid Father would get carried away and deliver a speech as if he were addressing a meeting, and Father had bowed to his advice.

Mr. Ivens would probably be the first to come to trial. A provincial election was due in Manitoba, and there was talk of nominating him to run for the legislature. Maybe he'd be sentenced to prison and unable to campaign, but a lot of people would vote for him, and he might even walk right out jail into the provincial legislature.

In his letter, Father used a phrase: *"Ivens versus the King,"* that puzzled Grace. She knew from Latin class that "versus" meant, "against". The king was George V of England, who lived faraway across the ocean and whose picture was at the front of her classroom. How could nice Mr. Ivens, their friend from Winnipeg days, be against the King of England, whom he'd never even met? If he were against anyone, it was employers who didn't pay their workers a fair wage. If Father was brought to trial, would he too be "versus the King"? How ironic, when in Winnipeg days the neighbourhood tough boys said he looked like the king.

She consulted Mother, who explained that Canadian courts used that wording because Canada was a former British colony. In the United States, she said, it was "versus the People." That formula didn't fit Father's situation either, for many of the "people" supported the stand he'd taken.

The thought of his trial hung over the family like a dark cloud, but the rain never came. As the months passed, as Father wrote cheerful letters home, Grace and the other children relaxed.

It was fall before Father came home again. Bruce had started school, Mother was back teaching, Charles and Ralph were taking violin lessons, and everyone was all right. On the day he was due to return, the whole family, along with Anna, Kathy and their families, and other well-wishers, came down to the government dock to meet the Vancouver boat. Suddenly Grace realized that Charles wasn't with them. Where was he? Probably with his friends somewhere in the crowd. Mother didn't seem worried about him.

The steamboat docked, the gangplank was lowered, and among the disembarking passengers was a thin, bearded, grey-haired man carrying a worn valise.

"It's Father!" cried Belva.

Then they heard the strains of a violin. Everyone turned and there was Charles, who had stepped out from the crowd and was playing a tune to welcome Father home. It was "God Save the King."

Grace started to giggle. "God Save the King" didn't seem quite appropriate to honour a man who had been charged with being "versus the King." Of course, Charles didn't know many tunes yet, and he'd probably chosen "God Save the King" because it was always sung on important occasions.

Tears streamed from Mother's eyes as she stepped forward and threw her arms around Father. They hugged right there on the dock in front of everybody. Then came embraces all around, although Howard was a bit shy. Many people wanted to shake Father's hand and welcome him home. After greeting them all, the family walked back to Stonehurst, where tables were set up outside and a feast awaited them.

Before the dessert course, Dr. Fred asked Father to make a speech, so Father got up and said he had good news. He'd had a letter from the Attorney General of Manitoba informing him that the Crown intended to enter a "stay" in his case. Grace had read of prisoners on death row being given a "stay of execution" – a postponement till new evidence could be investigated. In Father's case, a stay meant that he wouldn't have to stand trial. The charges had been dropped, it seemed, although in theory he could be brought to trial at any time. But the strike leaders' defence lawyer thought that this was the Crown's way of saving face, since it was doubtful that the charges against Father would hold up in court.

As Grace clapped her hands, she wondered if it was safe now to bring home the contents of the Secret Vault.

CHAPTER TWENTY-ONE

A few days later, when the excitement over Father's homecoming had died down, Grace found him reading on the veranda.

"I have something to show you in the woods," she said. "Come on!"

"In the woods?" he said, rising from his chair. "Do you have some wild thing held captive up there?"

"No, Charles is upstairs."

Her father laughed.

"Are you taking food to some war resister who doesn't know it's over?" he asked.

She shook her head, and led him through the garden and up the trail. The wind rustled the branches and lifted their hair.

"I always enjoy a walk in the forest," Father remarked. "Is the surprise some new species of plant?"

"You'll see," she called over her shoulder.

"What's in that sack you're carrying?"

"You'll see."

The burlap bag contained a trowel for digging out the Secret Vault; that is, if she could recall where the breadbox was hidden. She hoped the red ribbon was still tied to the cedar tree. She hadn't been up here in months for fear of leading someone to the hiding place. Whenever the children suggested a hike, Grace always took them on a different trail.

Ah! This looked right. A cedar was leaning out over the trail, and there was the faded ribbon dangling from a branch. And there was the fallen log. There was no sign that the moss around it had been disturbed. She knelt, pulled away the vegetation, digging until her trowel struck metal. The bread box glinted in the sun. Father knelt beside her and together they lifted it out of its hiding place.

"What's in here?" He pulled off the lid, then unfolded the oilcloth.

"My books!" he exclaimed. "All safe. Who had the good sense to hide them here?"

"Kathy and I did, to keep them safe for you." Grace dusted the dirt off her hands. "It was Mother's idea to hide them. Mother thought the Royal North West Mounted Police might come and search the house for books that the crown prosecutor could use against you. But your case hasn't come to trial, and doesn't seem likely to, so it seems safe for you to have your books back again."

Father picked up each volume and looked at it with affection. Then, struggling to speak, he turned to Grace.

"How did you carry this heavy box up here?" His voice sounded choked.

"Kathy helped me."

"Things must have been hard on you. You must have been afraid."

Grace got a big lump in her throat. She swallowed and said, "Maybe a little bit."

Her father hugged her.

"I've asked so much of you children and your mother." His voice was shaky.

"It was a small thing to do. I believe in everything you stand for and was glad to try to help. I love you."

Father got out his handkerchief and wiped his eyes.

"I love you too," he said. "It goes without saying that I love all you children. I'm really glad that you believe in my work because I intend to continue."

"I hope you won't get arrested again."

"I hope not too. I don't think I'll face any bad consequences as a result of the strike."

"Was the strike worth it?" she asked.

"Those six weeks will make history," he said. "Business and government leaders saw people's needs can't be ignored. There is tremendous sympathy and goodwill towards the strikers all over Canada and it's the perfect time to build on that support and talk about change that will make people's lives better."

"It sounds as if you'll be going away again." Her tone was matter-of-fact.

He nodded. "Yes. I'll be on a speaking tour. And some people say I should run for public office. A workers' party is being formed in Canada – The Independent Labour Party – like the one in England, and I intend to be active in it."

"Would you run for a seat in the British Columbia legislature?" she asked.

"Maybe. Maybe even for the federal Parliament in Ottawa."

Grace blinked. "Really?"

He met her gaze. "You say you support my principles and I'm glad, because if I run for office I'll be called plenty of bad names. It may be hard on you children and your mother."

"We can handle it. We've had practice."

Thoughts were whirling in Grace's head. If Father were elected to the B.C. Legislature, would the family have to move to Vancouver? Leave the Landing? The idea that he might run for the federal Parliament was almost too big to deal with. If he got elected and went to serve in Ottawa, would the family move there? Living in Ontario, she'd see her relatives on Mother's side of the family more often.

Well, as Mother often said, they'd cross that bridge when they came to it.

She took a deep breath.

"You'd make a good Member of Parliament."

Father smiled. "If it does happen, it won't be right away. It will be months or years from now. But the thought is exciting. And now that women can vote in federal elections, they'll be running for Parliament in Ottawa. Maybe someday you'll do that."

Grace laughed.

"I'm glad you think so highly of me, Father, but no. I have other plans for when I'm grown up."

He studied her.

"Oh? What are you going to be when you grow up?"

"A French teacher, like Mother. One of these years, when I'm old enough, I intend to go to Paris, now that the war is over."

Her father nodded.

"That's an interesting plan," he said. "Whatever you do, you'll be good at it."

Then he tucked the bread box under one arm, reached for her hand, and together they walked out of the woods.

EPILOGUE: 1966

Grace stood in front of her mirror, buttoning the jacket of the pink suit she'd bought on sale in Vancouver. She glanced at the clock on her dressing table, then fluffed her white hair to give it more volume. Taking a deep breath, she told herself to calm down. Yes, today was special, but at her age, she'd already enjoyed a lot of red-letter days.

Sitting down, she picked up her lipstick, then paused to look at the pictures that sat on her dressing table or were tucked into her mirror frame. She'd always liked the one of herself taken in her father's office on Parliament Hill when she was in her early twenties and working as his unpaid assistant.

She'd never expected to have a life in politics. After university she went to Paris, where she perfected her French, fell in love and had her heart broken. On returning to Winnipeg where the family was living, she'd taught French in the public school system, but, unlike Mother, she'd hated it. She wasn't cut out to be a teacher.

She felt like an awful failure until Christmas, when Father came home from Ottawa. When he heard how much she'd disliked her job, he said, "Why not come to Ottawa and work for me?" So she had, and there she met her future husband, Angus, a Member of Parliament in her father's caucus.

Here was Angus, in this historic 1933 photo, with Father and a crowd of people at the founding convention of a new political party, the Cooperative Commonwealth Federation, the C.C.F., in Regina. And here was a picture of her parents together, white-haired but still healthy-looking, taken sometime in the 1930s – before 1939, the year the Second World War started.

She well remembered the September 1939 Parliamentary debate over whether Canada should follow Britain's example and declare war on Nazi Germany. It was a foregone conclusion that a majority of Members of Parliament would vote to go to war against Hitler, Angus among them. Out of respect, though, the members of the C.C.F. caucus let Father speak first and express his belief in peace.

She felt a stab of pain, remembering the fragile white-haired man tracing the downward spiral of events toward this Second World War, which had come about partly because the countries of the world hadn't tried hard enough to make the League of Nations work. What her father said was true and accurate, but even so, she and Angus believed that Hitler had to be stopped. Yet she was proud that her old father had dared to stand alone and risk condemnation for his lifelong belief in peace.

She peered at another picture, this one from the early 1940s, showing the C.C.F. members of the British Columbia legislature, including a pretty, dark-haired woman – her younger self. What a strange, hectic time that had been – wartime again – she and Angus having to live apart from each other for several months of every year, because he had to go to Ottawa to represent his constituents, and she had to be in Victoria, representing hers. Meanwhile, her father, disabled by a stroke, lived in Vancouver with Mother as his life gradually ebbed away.

A more recent snapshot in Grace's mirror frame added a dash of colour. It was of the family reunion last summer. Several of her siblings had fascinating, distinguished careers and all of them were good citizens living worthwhile lives. They didn't get together as often as they would have liked, but they kept in touch with each other and were proud of each other's successes.

The last picture, in a silver frame, was her twenty-fifth wedding anniversary photo. Now it blurred, for her eyes were full of tears. Angus, older than she, had been ill for several years before he died. Once, toward the end, he'd said that he'd held her back, first because of his career, and then because of his illness.

"No," she'd said, "that isn't so. I've had a wonderful life, mostly thanks to you."

"Promise me, that after I'm gone, you'll run for Parliament," he'd insisted. "All the work you've done over the years for the party shouldn't go to waste." And in the election just past, she'd won a Vancouver seat, and today she was being sworn in.

It was almost time for her to leave her apartment, take the elevator down to the foyer and meet the taxi which she'd booked to take her to Parliament Hill. As she picked up her purse, she heard a knock at the door.

Grace touched Angus's pictured face, then her father's, for good luck, and hurried to the door to see who was there.

"Belva!" she exclaimed. "Mother!" She smiled at the ninety-two year old woman leaning on her sister's arm.

"Mother insisted on seeing you before you go," Belva looked fondly at the old lady.

Grace bent to embrace her mother.

"Grace, you look lovely," Mother whispered. "Go, now, and make the world a better place."

AFTERWORD

G race Woodsworth MacInnis (1905-1990) was a remarkable Canadian who made a great contribution on social issues, particularly those pertaining to women. As a federal Member of Parliament for Vancouver Kingsway (1966-1974), she was the only woman in the New Democratic Party caucus and in the House of Commons for several years. The mantle of woman's spokesperson fell on her shoulders by default, and she took it on with energy and enthusiasm.

As a student at Queen's University during the early 1970s, I admired Mrs. MacInnis whenever I saw her on television. This tiny white-haired woman, who often wore a pink suit and looked quite conventional, took an outspoken and progressive stance on issues of concern to young women like myself who hoped for a wider, more autonomous role in the world than previous generations of women had.

Years later, I co-authored a biography of Grace MacInnis, (*Grace MacInnis: A Woman to Remember*, Xlibris, 2000) a project involving many pleasant hours researching her life. Grace's early family life as the daughter of Lucy Staples Woodsworth, a teacher and supporter of causes relating to child welfare and peace, and James Shaver Woodsworth, the founder of the C.C.F. Party (forerunner of the N.D.P.) developed her social conscience and gave her convictions and courage.

Many Canadians have heard of the 1919 Winnipeg General Strike and are aware that J.S. Woodsworth was involved in it. At the time, Grace and her siblings were with their mother in Gibson's, B.C., reading newspaper accounts of this major labour action and worrying about their father being in the thick of it. I have tried to capture in this novel the challenges they faced, growing up in turbulent times with their father often away trying to make the world a better place.

Most of the family incidents in the story really happened, but not necessarily in the order or time frame in which I have presented them. A few events and some secondary characters are fictional creations. I have also created scenes, used dialogue and added some fictional letters. Consequently, this book is not a biography, but a work of fiction – a novel. The part about the secret vault, however, is absolutely true.

Ruth Latta

BIBLIOGRAPHY

Archival materials:

The J.S. Woodsworth Papers, Library and Archives Canada, Ottawa, MG27 III c7, Vol. 15, 16.

Grace MacInnis Papers, Library and Archives Canada, Ottawa, MG32 C12, Vol. 1-24.

The CCF (Cooperative Commonwealth Federation) Papers, Library and Archives Canada, MG28. IV. 1.

Diary of Grace and Angus MacInnis, Special Collections, University of British Columbia Library.

Interviews with Grace MacInnis from Archival Sources:

Covernton, Jane, Interview with Grace MacInnis, April 23, 1973, British Columbia Provincial Archives, Victoria, B.C.

Scotton, Anne, Interview with Grace MacInnis, April 1978. University of British Columbia, Special Collections.

Stursberg, Peter, *Transcript of a Series of Nine Interviews with Grace MacInnis, Vancouver, November 17, 1979,* Oral History Project, Parliamentary Library and Public Archives of Canada.

Other interviews:

Mills, Allan, Interview with Grace MacInnis, October 1983, *Manitoba History,* Number 7, Spring 1984.

Trott, E. Joy, Interview with Grace MacInnis, Vancouver, B.C., October 24-26, 1986, used with permission of the late E. Joy Trott.

BOOKS:

Blanchet, Muriel Wylie, *The Curve of Time,* Toronto, Whitecap Books, 1966.

Bumstead, J.M. *The Winnipeg General Strike of 1919: an illustrated history,* Winnipeg, Winnipeg Arts Council, 1994.

Dale, Stephen, *Noble Illusions: Young Canada Goes to War,* Halifax/Winnipeg, Fernwood Publishing, 2014.

Dwyer, Gwynne, *Canada in the Great Power Game,* 1914-2014, Toronto, Random House, 2014.

Heron, Craig, ed., *The Workers' Revolt in Canada,* 1917-1925, Toronto, University of Toronto Press, 1998.

Keller, Betty C., and Leslie, Rosella M., *Bright Seas, Pioneer Spirits: The Sunshine Coast,* Victoria, Horsdal and Schubart, 1996.

Latta, Ruth and Trott, E. Joy, *Grace MacInnis: A woman to remember,* Philadelphia, X-libris, 2000.

MacInnis, Grace, *J.S. Woodsworth: A man to remember*, Toronto, Macmillan, 1953.

McKay, Ian and Swift, Jamie, *Warrior Nation: Rebranding Canada in an age of anxiety*, Toronto, Between the Lines, 2012.

MacMillan, Margaret, *The War that Ended Peace: the Road to 1914*, Allen Lane, Penguin, 2013.

McNaught, Kenneth, *A Prophet in Politics: A Biography of J.S. Woodsworth*, Toronto, University of Toronto Press, 1959.

McNaught, Kenneth, *J.S. Woodsworth*, (The Canadians series) Toronto, Fitzhenry and Whiteside.

Mills, Allen, *A Fool for Christ: the political thought of J.S. Woodsworth*, Toronto, University of Toronto Press, 1991.

Peterson, Lester R., *The Gibson's Landing Story*, Ottawa, Peter Martin Books, 1962.

Steeves, Dorothy Gretchen, *The Compassionate Rebel: Ernest Winch and the growth of socialism in Western Canada*, Vancouver, J.J. Douglas, (c) 1960, 1977.

Woodsworth, Charles J., *A Prophet at Home: An intimate memoir of J.S. Woodsworth with three of his previously unpublished letters*. (Vancouver, Tricouni Press, 2005).

ARTICLES

Pritchard, W.A., "The 1919 Winnipeg General Strike", *The Western Socialist*, Vol. 36, No. 269, No. 3, 1969.

Hodordyski, Mary, "Women and the Winnipeg General Strike of 1919" *Manitoba History*, Number 11, Spring 1986.

MacInnis, Grace, "J.S. Woodsworth – Personal Recollections", *Manitoba Historical Society Transactions*, Series 3, Number 24, 1967-68.

Naylor, Jim, "The Winnipeg General Strike", presented at the conference, "Rekindling the Spirit of 1919" for the 90th Anniversary of the Winnipeg General Strike, May 19, 2009, published in *Canadian Dimension*, http://canadiandimension.com/articles/2320.

Rosner, Cecil, "What the Journalists Were Saying", a review of Michael Dupuis, *Winnipeg's General Strike, Reports from the Front Lines*, (History Press, 2014, reviewed in *Our Times*, Oct.Nov. 2014 issue.

BIO NOTE

Ruth (Olson) Latta has a Master of Arts in History from Queen's University, Kingston, Ontario. For many years she taught creative writing courses in Ottawa. *Grace and the Secret Vault* is her third young adult novel and her eighth novel.

For more information about these works of fiction as well as her non-fiction books, please visit her books blog at http://ruthlattabooks.blogspot.com.

She lives in Ottawa with her husband, Roger Latta, and her cat. Contact her at ruthlatta1@gmail.com.

www.ingramcontent.com/pod-product-compliance
Lightning Source LLC
Chambersburg PA
CBHW071434260626
47170CB00008B/2716